MW00710504

John W. Anderson

"Clutch"

Bootlegging, Love and Tragedy in the 1920s

By John W. Anderson

Illustrations by Barb Pearson

Copyright © 2003 by John W. Anderson

All rights reserved. No part of this book shall be reproduced or transmitted in any form or by any means, electronic, mechanical, magnetic, photographic including photocopying, recording or by any information storage and retrieval system, without prior written permission of the publisher. No patent liability is assumed with respect to the use of the information contained herein. Although every precaution has been taken in the preparation of this book, the publisher and author assume no responsibility for errors or omissions. Neither is any liability assumed for damages resulting from the use of the information contained herein.

This is a work of fiction. Names, characters, places, and incidents either are the product of the author's imagination or are used fictitiously. Any resemblance to actual events or locales or persons, living or dead, is entirely coincidental.

ISBN 0-7414-1720-0

Published by:

PUBLISHING.COM

519 West Lancaster Avenue
Haverford, PA 19041-1413
Info@buybooksontheweb.com
www.buybooksontheweb.com
Toll-free (877) BUY BOOK
Local Phone (610) 520-2500
Fax (610) 519-0261

Printed in the United States of America

Printed on Recycled Paper

Published October 2003

CHAPTER ONE

Jim Doyers mother, Elizabeth had died during childbirth. She had been weakened by severe hemorrhage, then shortly developed sepsis and lingered only two days before her death, without the benefit of a physician or hospital. She had only the services of the attending midwife, the older daughters and several neighbor farm wives. The newborn baby boy had died also. Elizabeth had earlier had pregnancies ending in miscarriages, and the couple had lost one infant son to scarlet fever. The father now struggled day to day, season to season, to feed and clothe his seven children; Priscella, age 12; Jim, age 11; Shane, age 10; Jeanie, age 8; Winston, age 6; Mary, age 4; and Amy, age 2. They all missed mother tremendously, every day. The older children had to intensify their labors, sometimes missing attendance at their nearby rural, one room school. They were bright children so they managed to move ahead one grade each year.

Their church of choice was nearby, of the Episcopal Synod. It offered them spiritual strength. Only Jim had to be coerced to attend Sunday school. He had been increasingly rebellious since the death of his mother. His father, Lee, had been finding it difficult to get him to perform a fair share of the fieldwork and the livestock chores. He would loiter on the way home from school each day, often engaged in mischief with some of the boys of his same tendencies. Who damned near burned down the schoolhouse on Halloween? Everyone in the neighborhood had strong suspicions. Jim's dad paddled the boy on more than one occasion, behind the wood shed with a rigid board. Jim's behavior would improve for a while, than soon regress to a lower level than previously.

Lee chose second wife, Ann Borrow, two years after his first wife died. She had lost her husband in an accident with runaway horses about the same time Elizabeth had died. Lee had been farming her land for her ever since. She was younger with only two children, a boy, Kim, now age 3, and a girl, Helen, now age 2. The mother and two children had been spending a great deal of time at the Doyer's so it seemed good sense for Lee and Ann to get married and raise all of the kids under one roof. Lee kept farming both quarter sections and they rented out Ann's house to a young hired man and his bride. Ann was an excellent gardener. All of Lee's children enjoyed the improved food on the dinner table. In fact Lee's children relished Ann and Ann's children loved Lee. There was one exception, Jim. He seemed to love no one. He just did not fit in. He and his father were constantly at each other.

Jim received his Eighth grade diploma the next spring. There was a reception party that night at the school. It was late when the Doyers got home, all turning into bed tired. Jim was nowhere to be found the next morning. At first everyone thought he maybe had slipped out during the night to join one or more of his friends for some all night frolic. Not so! He had run away in the dark of the night.

He had left the house shortly after midnight, when he was sure everyone was asleep. Heading straight east, across fields, staying off paths and roads to avoid detection. When he reached a branch of the Mouse River he remained secreted in the cotton wood grove along its banks right up to the town of Bergen. By that time it was into the afternoon. He had helped himself to a few radishes and strawberries out of farmer's gardens, but he was still hungry. There was very little other produce ripe yet. He drank from several springs along the river. He had no money. He was reluctant to venture into the town, to beg, afraid the word may be out about his running away. He lay low by the railroad tracks on the edge of town waiting for a freight train to come by slow enough for him to catch it, hopefully headed southeast to Valley City. His plan materialized. He reached his destination that late afternoon, the train bringing him nearly

2

to the station. He bummed a dime from a passenger waiting on the platform, his youth making it hard to refuse. The dime bought him a bowl of soup and a sandwich, the best he had ever eaten. He slept all night on a park bench with newspaper for cover.

He started down the street job-hunting the next morning. Times were good in the post World War I United States. He had not walked one block when he saw a sign "HELP WANTED". It was a big warehouse. He walked into the office where they hired him without question. Age did not matter, though brawn counted.... Jim had plenty of the latter. The foreman, Joe, took a liking to Jim. He did not ask too many questions. Jim accomplished more than his share of work, loading and unloading heavy construction material in and out of trucks. There was no power equipment to assist with the job. There was no mid-morning break. By noon Jim was more than hungry. When a 12:00 o'clock whistle blew the crew all headed for the lunchroom. The men laid out buckets of ham sandwiches, fried chicken, apples, pickles, thermoses of coffee and other goodies. Jim had nothing. He hated to admit his poverty. He told the men he had forgotten his lunch. They all shared. That evening Joe asked Jim to come home with him. He suspected Jim was without food or shelter or clothing. He invited Jim to stay in his home. Their house had an extra bedroom, Joe's wife, Trudy, also made Jim feel at home. They had two children, Pete and Alice, ages 8 and 10, who thought it was great to have a guest. They asked only a small payment for the room and board, payable when he received his first check. After several days, they all got around to discussing Jim's running away. Joe and Trudy saw Jim's side of it.

The morning Jim was found missing from his home, his father, Lee, drove north to Voltaire with a wagon and team, stopping along the way to inquire if anyone had seen Jim, Voltaire always having been the town where the family did their shopping. He found no one that had seen Jim. Lee was remorseful. He loved Jim very much, in spite of their frequent confrontations. It was another heavy burden on his heart. As the days, then weeks, then months and years went by he feared he would never see his son again, something terrible must have happened to him. But then at the same time he kept up hope and if ever Jim did return, Lee would ask for forgiveness and treat Jim like a prodigal son. He would put his arms around his son and squeeze him tight, hoping his son would return the gesture and that tears would come to their eyes. Jim had never been a hugger, nor had his father. At this time he could not remember when he had hugged any of his children. Distance seemed to be better than closeness. Now with Jim gone he was reconsidering how to relate to his children. He was thinking about giving them all a hug tonight, including Ann and her two children. Maybe this would relieve some of the stiffness that had hung over the family since Jim had run away.

Jim felt very fortunate to have a home in Valley City with Joe and Trudy. He helped around the place in any way he could, mowed the grass, hoed the garden, washed the car, peeled potatoes and dried the dishes. He never went out carousing at night. The speakeasies probably would have allowed him entrance, because of his mature appearance, but Jim wasn't sure what he would have done after he got inside, strange territory to him. He bought a few one-cent novels at the newsstand. That and listening to the radio occupied his evenings. The long day's heavy work, 7:00AM to 5:00 PM, tired him early in the evening. His room, upstairs in the house, with only one window, would sometimes be unbearably hot in the mid-summer unless a breeze off the prairie would stir the air. On those nights the entire family would sleep on the front porch, open, not screened free access to the mosquitoes until there was not enough moisture to allow their survival. The city would then become mosquito free.

After one month on the job, Joe spoke to the owner of the warehouse about a raise for Jim. He had started at 25 cents an hour. The boss raised him to 30 cents. No extra overtime- pay, no perks in those days. The new raise brought him up to the level of several of the young men at work. Some who had been there for a couple of years had higher wages yet. Joe was obviously the top earner, but what wage? Jim never knew. He never saw Joe's pay envelope. The work schedule was six days a week. Payday was Saturday, in cash. Some of the men hit for the closest speakeasy, some would stop at a bowling alley or pool hall for some sport. Some who were family men would go home and drag their wife and kids to a silent movie palace. Jim generally went directly home to Joe's house. He spent many evenings with Joe and Trudy's children, Pete and Alice. He missed his own young siblings. He hung a tire swing from a high limb in the back yard. Alice and her neighbor friends were in it constantly. Jim and Pete visited the town dump one Sunday afternoon and found two small wheels, ideal for a scooter. Jim constructed a body and upright steering post from scrap metal and pieces of lumber. Two salvaged bolts and nuts served as axels. The bearings in the wheels were not the smoothest running in town, but with a little grease and forceful pushing from Pete's strong legs he reached high speed, particularly down hill on the several surfaced streets in town. Jim was a reliable "sitter", not that Joe and Trudy went out much anyway, occasionally to another young couples for a game of canasta. Church services and socials were for the family. Joe, Trudy and the family were good attendees. Jim held back. He felt uncomfortable in church, always had. His parents had forced him to Sunday school and Sunday services, but his dad, Lee, had given up after Elizabeth died. Jim had not been inside a church since his mother's funeral. He felt the Lord had let him down when he took his mother.

Jim was not a spendthrift, very little for recreation, a few clothes, cheap magazines and books, his room and board. That was it. Everything else went into a tin box, hidden in the closet of his bedroom. Jim had thought about a car, nothing fancy, he did not have the money for that. The neighbors to the north of Joe and Trudy's place had an old unused barn on the back of their lot that Jim thought would be nice to use as an automobile shop. It even had an old barrel stove in it for heat. Jim asked about it. The owners agreed to let him use it, for pittance. Jim found an old Model-T Ford coupe with one wheel in the junkyard. It wouldn't run. It had no paint on it, had never seen a day under cover. The hood was gone, the tires were flat, and the headlights and the windshield were smashed. Its vintage was about 1919. The junk dealer practically gave it to Jim to get it out of sight. Jim had his friends from work push it home one evening, and deposit it in the barn. Jim stood and looked at it for some time, not knowing where to start with its restoration. Joe suggested working on the engine first. If that wasn't salvageable, there was no use working on the rest of it.

Jim had no automotive experience. His father had no power machinery, no tractor, no pump engine, and no feed mill. Everything was done by hand or with horses. The milking and separating were done by hand. Joe had a little hands-on knowledge, being called on at times to tune up the boss's trucks. On Sunday afternoon the two of them lifted the old model-T onto blocks and looked over the engine. It appeared to be intact, with no major parts missing. They proceeded to disassemble it; piece-by-piece, even removing the head, crank shaft and pistons. Several of the spark plugs were cracked. The coil appeared badly weathered. The crankcase contained only a smidgen of oil. The radiator was intact but appreciated a cleaning. The distributor, carburetor, generator and fuel pump were functional. Jim stopped at the junkyard Monday after work and picked up a coil and 4 spark plugs off an old wreck. Jim cleaned the engine block and all the parts with gasoline soaked cream separator brushes, till everything shined. The oil pan was found to have a hole in it. He patched it, using welding equipment at the junkyard. He replaced all of the wiring, picked up a few bolts and nuts at the hardware store for replacements where needed. Joe helped with the main reassembling. In two weeks it was ready for a trial. Jim nearly cranked his arm off. He flooded the engine. Joe said, "Let it sit for awhile". That was not easy to do. They went in for supper. Jim's arm was sore. His wrist was swollen from one kick back. After supper Joe said, "I'll give it a crank". One time and the engine caught, ground out a few sputters, and kept running. Jim reached in through the door and with one hand on the choke he feathered the engine into a nice regular purr. He advanced the throttle a couple of times speeding it up like a galloping horse. Jim had a smile on his face a mile wide. Joe slapped him on the back. Much more was needed to get her roadworthy but promise was now reachable. The doors and other panels were sanded till they shined like chrome. Jim painted the exterior with several coats of glossy black auto enamel, stroking his brush like and artist. Trudy helped with re-stuffing the coiled spring seat and recovering the seat and back cushion with black calf leather. The floorboards were replaced. The old horn still worked. Jim postponed replacing the windshield and the leather top. He felt he was getting too much money into it. Two tires were repairable, two had to be replaced from the junkyard stock. The original Ford tool kit and tire pump had been found in the truck. D Day (Drive Day) was fast approaching, scheduled for the last Sunday in September. Jim had difficulty locating replacements for the headlight lenses, finally having to order new ones from the Ford agency in Valley City. The first ones received were the incorrect size, requiring re ordering delay. The second and correct shipment arrived just in time to be installed for the big day. Fever, in anticipation of the inaugural run was running high in the neighborhood. It was the talk of the town. Jim kept the barn door locked except when he was working on the car. If open, the barn was full of men giving advice and at times even a little help. Kids were constantly crawling in and out of the car, until one rainy day, the muddied feet compelled Jim to put a stop to it. "No getting in or on the car and that means the trunk, also! Now scat."

Jim and Joe started up the engine several times; early the announced Sunday morning, tuning the carburetor, spark and choke. The noise attracted a good crowd. Even the minister from the church down the block stopped in and gave his blessing to his parishioners who he suspected were going to miss his sermon to be able to attend the launching. Jim had not named his car. It must be done, champagne or not. Then it came to him as he looked at the sky and saw nothing but clouds. "I christen thee "Cloud". It was to rain appropriately before the day was over. Jim was in the drivers seat with one foot off the clutch pedal. Joe was in the front at the starter crank. Jim said, "Let her go!" Joe answered, "OK" and gave the crank an almighty turn. The engine caught immediately. Joe jumped into the passenger seat. Pete and Alice were in the truck with the cover propped open. Jim eased his foot off the clutch pedal and moved it into the gearshift peddle, depressing it as he took his foot off the brake peddle. "Cloud" lurched forward, nearly dumping Pete and Alice out of the truck. Luckily they were hanging on with all their strength. Their mother, Trudy, was standing at a distance. She screamed, "Save my children." No one heard her. The car sped out of the yard into the street, where Jim took a sharp right turn. Only Joe's weight on that side prevented "Cloud" from tipping over right there on its maiden trip. Jim then remembered he could reduce the speed of the vehicle by easing off on the hand throttle. Prior to then he had been pressing on the brake pedal with all his weight as he said to Joe, "We are going to have to tighten the brakes." Joe said, "I guess so."

Cloud was responding nicely to the controls. Jim gained experience by the minute. The steering was on the loose side. That, with a tendency on Jim's part to over-correct his errors, led to a swerving path down the street. Stop signs were non-existent in Valley City at that time. Cloud slowed down very little at intersections. The biggest safety factor going for the entourage this Sunday morning was the scant amount of traffic. Few people owned automobiles. Those that did were in church. Several horse and buggy travelers spooked badly when Cloud came upon them, creating near run-a-ways, drivers shaking their fists at Jim and Joe as they sped by. Jim headed for Depot Street, pulled over to the side, and stopped. He had some trouble commanding Cloud to hold. She wanted to creep ahead. The clutch and gear pedals were a bit out of phase. Jim did not want to kill the engine. What if they couldn't get it started again? They were a good mile from Joe's house, a long way to have to push if necessary. Jim wanted to give Joe a turn at the wheel. Joe jumped out of the passenger side, went around to the driver's side where he jumped in quickly as Jim took his foot off the brake pedal and slid himself over to the right. Joe had a few more learned driving skills than Jim did and handled Cloud very well. He drove away from the depot into the country where he could allow Cloud the thrill of full speed. She had no speedometer. It was a guess, but the estimate of the two men was somewhere near 30 miles per hour, a devil of a speed, a scare against losing control on the loose, dry dirt gravel and flipping the machine into the ditch. A rooster tail of dust rose into the sky behind. Joe quickly slowed down. They had already stampeded several herds of sheep, heading them towards their home barn. They passed several horses in pastures, the critters taking off wildly, ears pointed to the sky, eyes white with fear. Pete and Alice thrilled at every minute of their ride in the trunk, even while eating the billowing dust on the country roads. They stood up once looking over the top of the trunk cover to holler at Jim and their father, the men screaming at them to sit down before the car would hit a bump in the road that would throw them flying. Such a trauma would certainly be injurious, at the least covering them with dirt filled abrasions or worse; broken limbs or head injuries.

CLOUD'S trial run by Jim, with Joe in the passenger seat, kids in the trunk

The dashboard had no gas gauge, no gauges at all. The tank was full when they started, but the men had no idea how many miles or hours it would last. They stopped once to measure the gas level with a stick. The tank was getting low. They checked the level of oil in the crankcase. That was okay. They headed home, reaching their neighborhood to find Trudy staring down the street from the same spot she had been standing when they left. She was sure by now that there had been a terrible accident with her two children dead or at the least injured beyond recognition, laying, with identity unknown, in the local hospital, to where she was about to dispatch a friend to make inquiries. She screamed and ran towards Cloud when she saw the car turn the corner towards her. She did not see the children until the car stopped by her side. She wailed with a joyful but swollen heart, gathering the children together in one big bundle, eyes flooded with tears, overflowing down her cheeks. How much grief can a mother suffer? She recovered slowly, it being a long time before she could hear Jim and Joe exclaiming the wonders of Cloud and the glorious trip the car had given them. Trudy next fixed her attention on the dust covering the children, their eyes shining through their dirty masks like small light bulbs. She lifted up her apron and wiped away the worst of the dirt, dragging the children towards the house, promising them the best baths they had ever had. Neighbors gathered quickly, surrounding Cloud, Jim and Joe to hear of boisterous tales, embellished with pride and exaggeration. The estimated maximum speed climbed to 40 miles per hour, maybe 50 down hill. Jim's accomplishing the tricks of the clutch was a story in itself. Several men from the warehouse, where he worked, showed up. Jim had to retell the story to them, of his accomplishment of the intricacies of the Model-T Ford clutch. They sensed an element of braggadocio overshadowing his ebullience. They talked of this when they left, feeling they may have to bring Jim down a level or two. He was riding a little high.

Monday morning, when Jim entered the warehouse, to start work, he found he had acquired a new name. "Clutch." "Good morning Clutch!" "How's your car, Clutch?" "Will you help me move this box, Clutch?" He tried to act flattered. After a while it bored into him a little bit. It went on all day. Not one time was he addressed as "Jim."? By evening time he had become used to it. The nickname stuck. He was no longer "Jim Doyer." He was "Clutch Doyer." Even Joe, Trudy and their children gradually switched over to calling him "Clutch" in their home. The name was unusual. There were a lot of "Jims." He knew no one else by the name of "Clutch" The name had many connotations. It meant strength (in a clutch). It was easily identifiable with automobiles. He was soon wearing the nickname as a badge of honor, not really what his fellow employees had first intended. They had come on it as a suggestive smear.

He had Trudy buy an automotive license for Cloud that week. He had no desire to get picked up by the local police. Clutch took Cloud for a joy ride every evening. He had no trouble finding passengers, adults or children, the latter usually riding in the trunk. The trunk cover had been removed to make it more accessible. Clutch spent a lot of time working with the engine. He was never completely satisfied with its function. He learned the need and function of every part. One evening another Model-T owner stopped by, the stranger's auto was running poorly, no power, couldn't even climb a slight incline. He asked Clutch if he would take a look at it. He offered to pay. Clutch had his head under the hood about fifteen minutes, he told the owner to crank the engine. It caught immediately and roared like a mountain lion. The stranger asked, "How much?" Clutch said, "Fifty cents." The man paid and with a "Thank you." Clutch was in the automotive repair business.

The Model-T Ford was the most prevalent auto on the streets. More and more people were becoming owners. Henry Ford was perfecting the assembly line, being able to market his autos at an affordable price. Good mechanics were in big demand. The word about Clutch got out quickly. He had people at the barn every night asking him for service. He had little time to cruise around in Cloud. It was into the fall anyway, time to drain Cloud's radiator and put her up on blocks for the winter. He and Joe hauled in a pile of firewood for the barrel stove. A couple of good kerosene lanterns served as the light source. He was soon making as much money in the evening servicing Model-Ts as he was on his job at the warehouse. He started thinking bigger, maybe finding an old empty building in the commercial district of town, bigger and more weather proof than the barn, with better heat, maybe even electricity for better light and a few power tools. He kept a look out for such a property all fall and winter and inquired with several realty offices. Nothing showed up. Several building contractors heard of his search and came to him with proposals. Even though he had been reassured that financing was available from the bank where he had recently been depositing his money, giving up the security of the tin can in his closet, he was fearful of taking such a big jump. He was developing a larger and larger repair business. The neighbor's barn was totally inadequate. He had had hired another young mechanic, Sparky Olson, to work with him in the evening and on weekends. His full time job was in a gasoline station, where he had some experience with different autos than the Model-T. He had worked on Buick's and Chevrolets and had a service manual containing instructions for tuning and repair of the new Willis-Knight Automobiles. This additional experience and information further expanded the capabilities Clutch could provide to his customers. The neighbors yard in the vicinity of the barn was becoming jammed with autos waiting for work. Clutch had voluntarily increased his rent payment to the owners of the barn early in the winter.

Clutch had nearly given up on finding a vacant building and neared a decision to proceed with buying land and erecting a building when an old wagon maker died leaving his shop unoccupied. The heirs wanted a quick sale, as usual wanting to turn the property into cash, none of them being interested in the wagon making trade. They were willing to leave all of the tools and equipment. Clutch made an offer. It was refused. He upped it. They accepted.

It was a year since Clutch had ridden the rails into Valley City and found a job at the warehouse. He now went to his boss and told him he was going into auto repair and service full time. The boss immediately offered to double his wage if he would stay. Clutch, though now only sixteen years of age, had proved to be one of the most reliable and productive employees. There was something about Clutch that was different, a charisma that was hard to define, a "smooth" way of approaching problems and quickly solving them without any fanfare. The boss gave up trying to convince him to stay. He could see Clutch's mind was made up.

The most interesting feature of Clutch's year away from home was his location not having been found by his family back on the farm. Nobody in Valley City realized he was a lost person, that is, except Joe and Trudy, and they were too close lipped to utter a word. You would have thought somebody would have crossed paths with Clutch's father, Lee, or someone else in the Doyer family. To them it was still a mystery.

CHAPTER TWO

Clutch's plan for his business included Sparky. Clutch engaged Sparky in serious conversation the same Saturday evening he finished his job at the warehouse. Clutch said "Sparky, I want you to join me in the business as a full time partner. You could put a little money in yourself, if you have any savings, or if your folks want to stake you for a few dollars that would be O.K. Otherwise the bank has promised to lend me what I need to get going. My savings will be part of it. The building, its contents and the big lot are only costing me $200. I already have a pretty good selection of hand tools but we should have several of the more newly available electric power tools. We are going to operate on a strictly cash basis with our customers. No pay! No car! The sign on the building will read: ***Clutch and Sparky's - AUTOMOTIVE REPAIR,*** How about it Sparky? You do not have to answer me tonight." Sparky said, "Gee! That's a big offer. Sounds great. I have a few dollars in my savings account, same bank as yours. Let me think about it and talk to my folks about it. Are you going to talk to your folks about it? Clutch didn't say anything for a minute, and then said, "No, my folks aren't around here." Sparky thought best to ask no more questions. Sparky visited Clutch Sunday evening. They took Cloud out for a spin and stopped at the old wagon manufacturing building, talking over some other ideas Clutch had for the place. Sparky could not hold back his own enthusiasm. He committed himself right their to becoming Clutch's partner. They went to the bank together the next morning. Clutch had a second motive in wanting Sparky as a partner. Clutch was only sixteen, questionably of legal age. Sparky was eighteen. The banker liked that. Otherwise, Joe and Trudy's names were going to have to appear on the documents. Clutch had put down $25 of his own when he made his offer on the building. Sparky now threw in $10 of his own. The bank came up with the rest. Everyone agreed to terms of repayment, which came out to $10 a month for about two years. The closing with the sellers and buyers was scheduled for the coming Friday. Sparky finished out the week at the gasoline station. Clutch caught up on unfinished jobs in the barn, stalling off new customers until the business was moved to its new location. He arranged for ads in the VALLEY CITY GUIDE which offered Clutch and Sparky as specialists on clutches and spark plugs. He contracted a sign painter to compose a masterpiece with gold edged English scroll. Clutch obtained prices on several power tools, to include an air compressor. The old wagon maker had an electric drill press, which would prove invaluable. A metal lathe was also on the premises. Electricity for lights was the big plus. The building was even hooked up to city water and sewer. There was a crapper in a small cubicle in the back corner of the building. The building's location was perfect, just one block off of Main Street, convenient for people doing other business in town.

1925 AUSTIN/HEALY

Clutch and Sparky were very pleased with the business, more customers than they needed, but grateful for every one of them, all of them pleased with the quality of the work and satisfied with the charges. After several months the charge rates were increased some but still kept reasonable. After several months there was no problem with keeping up the bank payments so they asked for an accelerated payment schedule to $20 a month. This still left enough to pay their other bills, pay cash for the parts they required and leave a very adequate draw for both of them. Clutch voluntarily increased his rent payment to Joe and Trudy. He enjoyed the pleasure of a family home and particularly relished Trudy's home cooking. Cloud was driven to work all summer and fall being kept in the neighbor barn at night and parked in the back of the shop during the day. One of the customers took a liking to it and offered Clutch an outrageous price for it one day. It was sold on spot, cash. Clutch had a hankering for a new four seat Austin/Healy with a leatherette body. There were none in Valley City but he saw one pass through town one day. It was a beauty. He ordered one through the local dealer. It took four months to arrive. It became his pride and joy. He could take Joe's entire family in it for Sunday joy rides.

Clutch did not have a steady girlfriend. He had met several as neighbors and friends of Joe's and Trudy's, taken one to a movie palace a couple of times but then seemed to lose interest. His orientation was too strongly towards his business. He was not aloof, in fact very vocular, but the subject of conversation had to be of his choice and not trivial. There was interplay with Pete and Alice but even that was not frivolous but clearly on an adult level. On the other hand Sparky was in a serious relationship.

Trudy usually would not have supper on the table until about 7:30. There was a pool hall a block away from the shop, up on Main St. Clutch stopped there one day at the invitation of his parts suppliers. There was a small back room where a few favored customers could buy a glass of home brew or a slug of corn liquor. There was even a piano keyed by a black man playing boogie-woogie. Clutch enjoyed the diversion. He took up the habit of stopping there often. Clutch had never played pool. His friend offered to instruct him. Clutch was a natural. He soon developed skill to take on all comers. He made some new friends. It was a hang out for local businesses men as well as traveling salesmen. He made a particular effort to visit with a man, Fiagio (Fig) Corcione, who came through Valley City every month, representing a tool manufacturing firm out of Milwaukee, WI, traveling by train and usually staying over in the city one or two nights. This newfound friend seemed to know what was going on in the business world. He was very enthusiastic about the commercial climate in southern Wisconsin. Clutch visited with him again the next month becoming intrigued with what he was being told. Fig told him he should move to Wisconsin, not too far north of Chicago, and open up a new automobile repair shop. He could charge twice the prices he was getting in Valley City. He knew the right city for Clutch, Janesville, between Madison and Chicago. Fig, without detailed explanation, promised Clutch immediate financing to construct a state of the art repair shop and customers galore to ask for service.

Clutch was restless. He needed another challenge. Sparky had become married in May. His wife was already pregnant. Clutch was reasonably sure Sparky would buy him out. Clutch thought about the grandiose picture painted by Fig. He thought about it several days. He went for a long walk one evening after the shop had closed for the day. The sun was setting, pausing just above the horizon, as it seems to do early in the summer, and then setting quickly, followed by a lasting period of dusk. It went through his thoughts that this passage of light could be guiding his life. Where was he headed? Should he allow himself to be so guided or be stuck in the sky without movement? He made up his mind that evening to talk to Sparky. The next evening he offered Sparky a ride home. He divulged his plans and made Sparky an offer he could not turn down; buy clutch out for only half of what they had in the business, the original cost of the building plus what they had made in the way of other capital investment, plus a few accounts receivable. No "Blue Sky." Furthermore, Clutch did not want the money in a lump sum, but would accept a contract with monthly payments. Sparky was shocked at Clutch's plans. He then said, "I do not want you to go. How can I manage without you?" Clutch said, "You will do fine. We have one helper now. Get another one, and then another one, and soon you will be on easy street." Sparky said, "I will have to talk to my wife and folks about it" Clutch said "The next time Fig comes to Valley City I am going to go back to Wisconsin with him to look things over. When I get back, we can both make a decision."

Clutch made the trip back to Wisconsin with Fig the next time Fig had been to Valley City. They rode the Northern Pacific Railroad, two days and a night, in a Pullman Car, with their seats making up into two births at night, Clutch in the upper, Fig in the lower, passing through Minneapolis, and Saint Paul, Minnesota in the middle of the night. They spent part of their time in the Club Car, playing cards with several other men and having a drink out of the inside pocket of Fig's suit coat. Clutch had very little experience with cards, particularly poker. Fig and the other men were kind to him, though, choosing five card stud with the chips worth only one cent, a five cent bet limit and a limit of three bumps. No one got hurt and they all had a good time. Dinner in the diner was fancy, monogrammed china, plated silverware, crystal glassware and linen napkins. The menu was elegant. Clutch had raspberry pie for desert, following that cigars and fingerbowls. Clutch slept well. Fig rode right to Janesville with Clutch. He had telegraphed ahead to a friend about bringing a guest. The friend, Lago Vitorio, met them at the station. He said to Clutch, "Call me Lag." He carried their luggage to his auto, a shiny new two-seated Wembley with a huge trunk. Fig had checked his sample cases onto the baggage car. They picked those up in the freight room. Clutch had noticed as they drove away from the station that Lag's auto had more speed and power than you would have expected. Clutch said, "Boy this car has power." Lag said, "It's supercharged."

They drove right to a hotel downtown; five stories high, bellhops at the door, and crystal chandeliers in the lobby. After Fig and Clutch had checked in, Lag told them they were having dinner with his boss, Sigarto (Sig) Bellagio in the hotel dining room at 7:00, and before that at 6:30 were going to meet him in the men's lounge behind the dining room. After giving them the messages, Lag departed. So far, Clutch was impressed. Clutch and Fig had time for a bath and a short rest before they were to meet Sigarto. Clutch asked no questions of Fig. He figured his puzzlements would soon be clarified. Fig had to identify himself and Clutch at the locked door of the men's lounge. He spoke through a small opening in the door. It was then opened. They were ushered to a table where a middle aged, dark complexioned, mustachioed man was already seated. He arose courteously. Fig introduced him. "Don Sigarto Bellagio, this is Mr. James Doyer." Don Bellagio said, "Call me Sig." Clutch said, blushing some, "My nickname is Clutch. It's a long story but, my name has to do with my ability to repair and service automobiles."

They all sat down. Don Bellagio introduced the matter at hand by responding, "Yes, I understand you are an excellent automobile mechanic. Mr. Corcione has told me all about you in Valley City, North Dakota. He has also told me about the possibility of your moving here to Janesville. My organization has a number of automobiles. Our work demands that they can be in tip-top shape at all times. It is often necessary to have to drive them very fast. We have difficulty obtaining good mechanic work. I would be interested in building you a complete shop with all the necessary equipment here in Janesville. You wouldn't only have people in our organization as customers but all of our friends as customers. You would be very busy. You could pay me back the money month by month. When the debt is satisfied you would be given the title to the property." Clutch asked, "Don Bellagio, (Sig was pleased with him addressing him as 'Don') who will determine what I charge for my services?" Sig said, "You will of course. No question." Sig said "Think about it young man. We will meet here again tomorrow noon for your answer. Now, lets go to the dining room, enjoy a nice dinner as my guests and forget all this heavy business." Through this entire meeting, Fig had said nary a word. "By the way, Clutch, your room and the train trip are on me too." Clutch thanked Don Bellagio graciously as they were seated in the dining room. They all ordered the top item on the menu, 'Beef au juice'. Fig and Clutch had a green salad, twice baked potatoes, green peas and fresh rolls. Don Bellagio had only pasta covered with tomato/cheese sauce as his side dish with the beef. The waiter poured them glasses of Port wine, hiding the bottle under the tablecloth. They all finished up the meal with Neapolitan ice cream glazed with Galliano liquor, then a demitasse of strong Sicilian coffee. It had been an exceptional fare. Don Bellagio hugged both Fig and Clutch when they thanked him and bid "Goodnight".

Clutch and Fig were alone in the elevator when they ascended to their room. Clutch said, "My! Sig is a fine man. What is his business?" "He is in the delivery business", said Fig. "Delivering what?" said Clutch. Fig whispered in Clutch's ear, "Merchandise. No more questions." Clutch asked Fig, "Are Sig's predictions about the amount of business I'll be having true?" Fig answered, "For sure, and it wont be Model-T flivers. It will be on big cars: Buick's, Studebaker's, Rios, Chryslers, you name them. Do you know anything about super-charging cars, Clutch?" "Not much, but I can learn."

Clutch did not sleep well that night. He had all of this on his mind. He had a strong notion about what "merchandise" was. Prohibition had been enacted in 1919. It had reduced the consumption of alcohol in the United

States but had not eliminated it. The Federal Government was trying to enforce the law, forcing the liquor industry under ground. That had to be Don Sigarto Bellagio's 'Delivery Business'. Everything is adding up; his Sicilian name, his driver's name, even Fig's name, Fiagio Carcione, also Fig's monthly visit to Valley City. "He was peddling bootleg booze." Clutch thought to himself, "I wondered why he was always in the pool hall instead of the machine shops. I'll bet his huge sample trunks were full of whisky, not samples of tools. He must have peddled whisky right out of the baggage car to pool hall and speakeasy owners at every whistle stop between Milwaukee and Valley City, meeting them on the station platforms, stopping overnight in the larger cites where he had more customers. No wonder it took him a month to make a round trip. He would ask Fig about it the next day. Of course, Fig might not admit it if he was smart. Clutch eventually dropped off to sleep in a state of indecision, in the dark of the night.

Next morning, when Clutch got out of bed, bathed, dressed, had a cup of coffee in the hotel restaurant, then, the matter from the night before came clear to him. He would say to Don Sigarto Bellagio, "Yes! With your help, I am going to move to Janesville and open up the finest automotive repair shop in mid-America, which will give the best care available to you and your friend's autos and the autos of any other customers that want my services.' Clutch convinced himself that it would not be as though he himself were bootlegging the booze. Whatever, he would make enough money to live like a king. Fig came down and joined Clutch in the restaurant. He was told of Clutch's decision, and was pleased. Then Clutch asked him to explain the meaning of the term 'merchandise'. Fig admitted enough to confirm Clutch's conclusions. After breakfast, Clutch and Fig walked around town for several hours. The city was prospering. They came across several vacant lots that would lend themselves to the type of building Clutch had in mind.

Clutch was becoming excited about his new project. In spite of evidence for Don Sigarto Bellago being an underworld character, his confidence in Clutch seemed real and he came off as a man who would keep his commitments. Clutch felt if he played fair ball with him, Sig would do likewise. Sig, Fig, and Clutch were all on time for lunch. Not until they had finished their meal and were enjoying their coffee did Sig ask for Clutch's decision. Clutch's answer came out just like he had rehearsed it, 'Yes!' Sig said, "This will be for the benefit of both of us." Sig then asked Fig to telephone a man whose number he handed him, to ask if he was going to be in his office for the afternoon. "If he is, then tell him my driver, Lago Vittorio, will bring Clutch over there in a few minutes. "Clutch, he is a builder." I talked to him this morning about your plans. He will be honest, charging fair prices. He is one of "our family'. There will be no need to obtain bids. That will just delay the project. There were several potential locations he will show you. You tell him what type and size building you want and where you want it. Do not skimp. This will take up your entire afternoon. Tomorrow you and I are going to meet here at 8:00 for breakfast then, Fig, you and I are going to my attorney's office and draw up a contract for deed on the building, small payments to start with then accelerated later, as you wish. No one will push you. How does it all sound, Mr. Doyer?" Clutch exclaimed, "Great!"

Clutch had to pinch himself several times. Here he was to be only turning eighteen years of age a few weeks from now, but wheeling and dealing like an experienced man. He couldn't wait to tell someone, but whom. He would have to ponder that for a while. Now there was business at hand. The building contractor's name was Ian Shane. Be god, an Irishman, a jolly red-faced gentleman with a brogue. He called his draftsman into the meeting. Clutch told them he wanted it to be about 1500 square feet, small office up front, cement block walls with a furred up inner wall of plaster, well insulated (Clutch had enough of working in the cold), round roof, central heating, brick trim on the front. A toilet, wash sink and shower should be off the locker/lunch room. Clutch wanted plenty of windows, two hydraulic hoists, powered overhead hoist to lift engines, parts cleaning sink, a system to ventilate exhaust, high intensity lights, electrical receptacles for both 110v and 220v. He further said, I'll think of more later. Next, he and Ian went lot hunting. Interestingly, one of the lots was the same that Fig and he had noticed that morning. It turned out to be his preference. It was large, plenty of room to park cars awaiting service. The job was soon going to be under way. Clutch met Fig back at the hotel for supper after which they visited the local movie palace. It was a Harold Lloyd comedy, silent, but with an exceptional piano player in the pit.

Next morning's formalities did not take long, after which Sig went back to the hotel with Clutch, paid the bill, then took him to the train station, reimbursed Clutch for his train tickets with some extra for the meals, then said good bye. "See you in a month, Mr. Doyer. You will be surprised how much Mr. Shane's crew will have done by then." Clutch stopped off one day in Minneapolis to order tools and parts, stayed over in the Curtis Hotel one night, then back to Valley City the next day. He found Sparky as soon as he arrived in town, told him of the finality of his plan and told Sparky he now owned the Valley City shop all by himself. Sparky knew there was no point in balking. Clutch could invoke the buy-sell agreement in their partnership contract, Sparky would be out and Clutch would own it all. They met with their banker the next morning, which helped dissolve their partnership and prepare a contract for deed. Clutch put his beloved Austin/Healey up for sale and received an early offer. He did not have much else to do in Valley City. His belongings were few; he packed them in no time. The hardest part about leaving was saying goodbye to Joe and Trudy and their children. They had been his family and keepers. Joe stayed home from work the day Clutch left.

Clutch hired a Sedan and driver from the livery to drive them all to the station. The train was on time, no room for long goodbyes. When Clutch was ready to climb aboard he hugged both Pete and Alice and pressed a $10 bill into each of their hands. They screamed in delight. Clutch stopped over in Minneapolis again to check on his tool order. It was nearly ready to be shipped. He was pleased. He also bought some service manuals for both domestic and foreign cars.

CHAPTER THREE

Clutch was in Janesville the next day, much sooner than Don Bellagio had predicted. A visit to the building site revealed the new shop was already framed up. Exciting! Clutch found nice accommodations in a rooming house, meals included, only two blocks from his shop. The next afternoon he stopped at the post office and bought two-penny post cards and took them to his room where there was a small writing desk. He addressed one to Joe and Trudy, thanking them again. He hesitated before addressing the other, than wrote *Priscella Doyer, Rural Route 2, Voltaire, North Dakota.* Tears came to his eyes. All he said was, *"I have been in Valley City for two years working as an auto mechanic. Now I am in Janesville, Wisconsin. I have missed you very much. I am well. Are you and the family all right? My address here is PO Box 1452. Please write me. Love, Jim"*

Priscella was the one who walked down the lane to the mailbox each forenoon. There was usually something, catalogs, flyers, bills and **THE FARMER**. Today there was Jim's card, right on top. She picked it up, at first puzzled. Then she screamed, "Jims Alive!" She kept it up, all the way back to the house, running as fast and screaming as loud as she could. After all it was going into the third year since Jim had disappeared. Ann, the stepmother, her two children and Priscella's other five siblings were all in the house. It was near lunchtime. They had all been working in the garden all morning. Father Lee was out in the field where he was cultivating corn. He soon appeared by the barn, watering the team. Priscella hollered at him from the back porch. "Jim's Alive." He wasn't sure he had heard correctly. He put the horses in the barn, left their harnesses on, gave them each a quick pail of oats in their feed boxes and took off for the house in full stride. He read the card, not quite believing his eyes. Everyone was talking at once. He could not get a word in. He read the card again, then sat down at the kitchen table, tears in his eyes, sobbing quietly. He understood Jim's running away even less now. Soon his mood changed to joviality along with the others. Jim was alive and well. He had become an automobile mechanic. That is all they knew. It was a wonder.

Priscella wrote a long letter that evening, composing it very carefully, telling Jim everything that had happened to the family since he had left, which wasn't much, all getting older, of course, all in school but Ann and Helen, and herself, now graduated. Priscella had a boyfriend, the same age, the oldest child of a new family that had moved into the old Morgan place down the road. Priscella had been working some for Mrs. Cliburn, a half mile away, helping her can fruits and vegetables, she not having any children. Shane helped Mr. Cliburn cultivate and might stay on as a steady hand. Priscella and Shane often ate and slept at the Cliburn's. Supper at the Doyer's that evening was a joyous feast in celebration of the resurrection of their Jim. The next forenoon, Priscella took her letter and two cents down the lane and sat in the ditch grass waiting for the mail carrier. When he stopped, she told him of the card from Jim, gave him her letter and the two cents for postage, asking him to be extra careful with it. He promised her letter would receive special treatment. Two days later on Sunday morning, they all sat together in their family pew with smiles on their faces that fellow parishioners had not seen for over two years.

Jim was not quick to send another card. It seemed to him that he had little more to write, when the truth of it was, each week in his life was a new chapter. When he did get around to responding to Priscella's letter it was just another penny post card. She responded with another letter, asking Jim many questions, which he never did answer. His much chaptered life was a closed book. The postcard/letter, back and forth style, never changed.

Everyone in Janesville called Jim, Clutch. He was known as Jim at the farm and in Voltaire, where the nick name, Clutch, had never been heard of. He even thought of changing his legal name to Clutch but didn't get it done. The shop building was completed with unusual speed. A grease pit was in the plans. The concrete floor was poured and the roof was on in just over a month from the beginning of construction. The two hydraulic hoists were installed soon after. Clutch advertised for two mechanics at top starting wages. He had a large number of applicants. He settled on two that had experience working on big cars. Sig arranged a trip to Chicago for Clutch where he spent a week as a worker/observer in a huge garage. He worked on cars he had never heard of before. It was an encyclopedia of experience. He found out what service manuals he didn't have and made arrangements with several wholesale houses for parts he would need in his Janesville shop. He stayed in a YMCA, enjoying the experience of Chicago, but at the end of the week being glad to return to Janesville.

The new shop had not been named yet. Clutch wanted to incorporate his nickname in it as he had done in Valley City. He settled on:

THE CLUTCH SHOP--THE BEST FOR ALL AUTOMOTIVE SERVICE AND REPAIRS

CLUTCH DOYER-PROPRIETOR

He went to the best sign maker in Janesville. Clutch ordered it big, three feet wide. The tools he had ordered in Minneapolis had started to arrive. He had ordered more in Chicago. They were arriving also. Then contractor, Ian Shane hired a cabinetmaker to make cabinets and benches to fit along all of the walls. Lights were hung over all work areas and benches. The exhaust system was the best. The furnace was natural gas. The windows were from the highest-class sash and door firm in Wisconsin. Clutch was becoming a bit concerned over the costs. He met with Don Sigarto Bellagio. He reassured Clutch that there was no problem. A telephone was installed in the office of the shop. Calls starting coming in asking about an opening date. Clutch promised them a call back in a few weeks. There were three newspapers in town, two weekly, one daily. They all visited Clutch, getting information to write stories about his enterprise. They even wanted to know who was financing him. He didn't tell them. They offered the services of their advertising departments. Clutch visited the newspaper's offices and participated in design of some beautiful layouts for the coming grand opening. Everyone was fascinated with Clutch's nickname, labeling it a real winner. Clutch contracted with one of the Minneapolis tool manufacturers to produce ten automobile tool kits, with **THE CLUTCH SHOP** name imprinted on the tools, to be given away in a door prize drawing at the grand opening. A German Polka band was hired to play for the day, free rolls and coffee were going to be served. Everyone within 50 miles of Janesville was going to know about the new shop.

Priscella had asked Jim in her letter what church he belonged to, if he attended Sunday services? He never answered her. He felt content with his choice of "freedom from religion" and felt no need to discuss it. Clutch had once read the story of the American Native, Sagoyewatha, who said to a minister, "You say there is only one God and one religion, the Christian Religion. Then why do whites differ about it and have many churches? Why do you not all agree? We understand you all study from the same book. How can we believe your White Man's Book, being so often deceived by the white people? Brother, we do not understand these things. But, we do not want to destroy your religion. We only want to enjoy our own. Brother, you have now heard our answer to your talk. I will come and take you by the hand and hope the Great Spirit will protect you on your journey." The minister turned and walked away, refusing to shake Sagoywewatha's hand. Clutch had on several occasions been invited to attend Sunday Services at the churches of new acquaintances he had made in Janesville. Out of courtesy and appreciation he had accepted. The sermons did not impress him, leaving him empty, doubting. Thereafter, he turned down invitations, and they ceased. He spent his Sunday mornings reading the newspapers and automotive service manuals.

The grand opening of the **CLUTCH SHOP** was a huge success. The crowd was immense. They ran out of coffee and rolls two times but were able to replenish supplies. Clutch and his two mechanics had already been working in the shop prior to the grand opening, on a limited basis, principally servicing the auto's of Don Bellagio's operation. Some of Sig's 'gang" were, by Clutch's definition, rather swarthy, of dark complexion. Their speech was of foreign accent. On the other hand they were polite and considerate and well dressed. Their cars were something else; new with big engines, all black in color, large trunks, big tires with heavy tread, five or six gears, and big headlights. The manufacturers were many: Auburn, Chrysler, Lincoln, Reo, one Buick, 1924, Model 50, with a 70 horse power engine, whose owner told Clutch he paid $2,280 for it. Some of the autos were foreign. They were real class: Alfo Romeo, Bugotti, and Lancia from Italy; Rolls Royce from England; Mercedes Benz and Dusenberg from Germany; Franchine and Citrion from France. It seemed that every driver craved distinction by having a different car. The problems to start with were not big, mostly tune-ups and small adjustments, easily handled by Clutch and his two assistants. The owners of the cars always paid cash, not a single check. Clutch went to the bank every afternoon. One day, as he made his deposit, the teller said, "You are going to have that shop paid for in no time." Clutch thought he had better buy a safe. His choice was a model so heavy it took a cart with a hoist to bring it into his office. The local business outside of Sig's gang took a little longer to catch on, but when it started there was no end. Word of mouth was the best advertiser. By the end of four months he had hired two more mechanics and a lady office secretary. She was needed to make customer appointments, order parts, keep records of time on each job, cost of parts, and appease waiting customers. This freed up Clutch to dig into some of the more difficult jobs himself. The tougher the problem, the more he enjoyed it. Installing superchargers and tuning them was his favorite work. He was good at it. Even the local Auto agencies referred some of their toughest jobs to **THE CLUTCH SHOP.** He was on a very friendly basis with the Ford, Chevrolet, Buick, Chrysler, Lincoln and other agencies. This relationship existed on the basis that Clutch reassured them he had no interest in taking on an agency himself.

Clutch was very friendly with his customers, suppliers, and even curiosity seekers but developed a buddy-buddy relationship with no one. He occasionally stopped at one of the local pool halls where liquor was available in the back room and where he would run into some of Sig's gang. They would pass on small bits of the details of their activities, never giving him a clear picture of the entire operation. It was apparent they bootlegged liquor not only outside the law but also under the cover of the law. The center for the illegal distribution of liquor to the mid-west had been Chicago during the first years after enactment of prohibition. It was under control of Gangsterism. Competition led to many gang murders. Racketeering became a dangerous business in Chicago. The Sicilian faction, Mafia, did not want to relinquish control of their distribution operation but were constantly being threatened by other factions. Murders were becoming more commonplace. Sigarto Bellagio was in the midst of it. John Dillinger and his like were on a rampage in the Chicago area. Dillinger had been sent to jail in 1924. Even from behind bars he was intensifying the force of his gang. Two of his cohorts, Baby Face and Pretty Boy Floyd were in charge.

Sigarto Bellagio met with them late one night in the behind-doors bar of the Palladium Ballroom. They formed a compact: Sig would move out of the Chicago area, north into Wisconsin, where he and his gang would be the sole providers of bootleg whiskey. Their realm would extend into northern Wisconsin, Minnesota and the Dakotas. Indiana, Illinois, Iowa, Michigan, would be the Dillinger Gang's domain, One concession to Bellagio; he would be permitted, unmolested to receive shipments up the Mississippi River, through the Illinois River, Des Plaines River and Chicago River, at times through the Chicago Canal in season, into Lake Michigan to Milwaukee, in winter time overland. This had been the traditional shipping lane for bootleg liquor from Southern Europe into central United States, ever since the enactment of Prohibition in 1919. The Bureau of United States Treasury, responsible for enforcement of the liquor law, had been very ineffective in interfering with this reliable route. Shippers of other goods from Southern Europe had devised methods of hiding the liquor in the packing of other goods that made the liquor undetectable. Add that to the attractive "pay-offs" to longshoreman groups, river barge operators, local law enforcement operators, and the illegal industry of importing liquor was thriving. Distribution of the booze to thirsty customers was also a thriving branch of the business. That is where Don Sigarto Bellagio's Milwaukee/Janesville gang came into the picture. Now immune from trouble and competition from the Dillinger Gang, their operation was thriving. Only in the summer would they have to put up with a small amount of two-of-a- trade rivalry from the Ports of Duluth, Minnesota and Superior, Wisconsin where a small amount of booze was being smuggled into the United States from some of the Canadian Provinces that were enjoying the availability of liquor under their own laws, varying considerably from those in the United States. It was not a well organized operation, mostly just sailors picking up few bottles at Canadian ports, carrying them in their personal belongings to Duluth or Superior where they would sell it to longshoremen who would in turn distribute it to speakeasies, pool halls and locked door dance halls. Sig Bellagio detested this interference with his monopoly. He passed on work to the Longshoremen's union that it had to stop. They were offered two choices; either become part of his loose-knit mob or go there own way and will suffer finding some of their buddies floating face down in the harbor some morning. Being of their own tough vintage, they ignored Sig's threats. Several weeks later, two longshoremen were reported missing, in the dark of night. Days later they were found bloated and floating, face down, one in the Duluth harbor, one in the Superior harbor. One week later, Sig met with head of the Longshoremen's Union. Thereafter, there was no more trouble, the booze from Canada going directly to Sig's men with a pay-off to both the sailors and the longshoremen. Everyone was happy with getting their cut. The consumers were happy with getting the best of liquors from Canada, Great Britian, and Northern Europe along with the choices from the Mediterranean countries. It was difficult smuggling liquor from Canada in the winter months when Great Lakes ship traffic came to a halt. The two US Customs border check points on routes into Minnesota, one at Grand Portage and the other at International Falls, were tightly controlled with inspections of cargo commonplace. To bypass the checkpoints meant traveling by dog sled through wild country in dangerous winter weather. Such methods were unreliable and costly in money and lives. Bootleg crossings of the US/Canada border further west in North Dakota and Montana were easier transversed but no syndicate of underworld henchmen existed there, the need for any volume of bootlegged liquor being too small. Sig solved the matter by organizing the summer shipment of liquor on the Great Lakes ships into a bigger operation, none of this penny-ante stuff of sailors carrying it in their belongings. Sig arranged for whole cases of liquor to be packed at its origin disguised as other goods, unrecognizable by law officers as liquor. It went right from the ships to the warehouses, only then unpacked for distribution to its destinations. The branch of

Sig's operation grew exponentially, undetected by the "Feds", just like his Mississippi operation, nearly rivaling it in volume.

The distribution system of all this smuggled booze from Europe into Wisconsin, Minnesota, and the Dakotas, every bit of it under control of Don (Sig) Sigarto Bellagio became centered in Janesville. The syndicate reaped huge amounts of money. Every henchman, every deliveryman, every law officer got more than their fair cut or pay-off. There was still a huge profit for the Don. He owned a beautiful home twenty-five miles from Janesville on lovely Lake Geneva where he lived with his wife Helene and his two children, Vizzini, a boy, age 6; and a girl Finora, age 5. Sig and Helene's marriage was impeccable. They lived in high style, but not high in society, their activites mostly secluded. They kept a stable of horses with their own riding paths through a wooded area along the lake. They had an inboard powered Chris-Craft, mohagany decked speed boat in the boat house, and two cars in the garage, one an Alfo Romeo for Helene, the other Sig's Wembley. The servant's quarters and their garages were separate buildings at the back of the property. A high hurricane fence surrounded the entire area. Sentry post houses were located on all four corners and at the gate.

Helene and Sig were both natives of Sicily. He had immigrated to New York with his parents as a small child. His father was Mafiosa. He was shot dead, young, in gang-warfare. Sig's mother returned to Sicily, but Sig, in his teens, returned to the United States with an uncle, entering the Mafiosa at a very young age, then given opportunity to enter the Chicago Mafia Family with enactment of Prohibition. Helene was Sig's teen sweetheart in Sicily who he never forgot. He had returned to Sicily, fulfilling his promise to Helene, where they were married in Sicilian Custom, in the church of the Bellagio Family by an honorable catholic priest. The wedding was followed by a feast and dance unequalled in all the provinces of the Island, the festivities

34

lasting for days. The new bride was a beauty to behold, welcomed by all of Sig's United States Mafia family, when the two disembarked the ship at New York City.

Helene spent summers in Sicily, Sig joining her for at least a month. They wanted their children, Vizzini and Finora exposed to native ways. Sig had bought a mountain home near his and Helene's native village. The family was held in great respect by the villagers and near by farmers. Regardless, no risks were taken. Guards were with the family constantly. The Bellagios never returned to the United States until the Wine Festivals were over in the late summer. It was a glorious time in Sicily. Vino-culture and making wine were the major industry of the area. Horseback riding throughout the countryside was a daily pastime, tiring but relaxing. Days would end with a swim in their pool. Dinner would follow.

Back in Janesville, Don Sigarto Bellagio's business ran smoothly. Automobiles were the exclusive vehicle for distribution of the liquor out of the warehouses in Milwaukee and Superior. Trains were used when long distances were involved like on Fig's route to Valley City. There were similar routes that went to Grand Forks, Minot, and Williston, North Dakota and Sioux Falls, Pierre and Rapid City, South Dakota. Automobiles were preferred for all other uses. They were speedy and elusive, could travel at any time of the day, nighttime being of preference. Particularly the larger cars, big wheeled and heavy could transverse any roads in all kinds of weather. Purposely there were no scheduled times to make deliveries. That would make it too convenient for some heroic local cop or sheriff's deputy to nab a delivery destined for a pool hall in his precinct or a country dance hall off a rural road. Every buyer had a contact man that was available twenty-four hours a day. The deliveryman would surreptitiously approach the contact man's house, headlights off. A knock on the door would awaken him to help unload the cases of liquor into his garage. They would be hauled to his employer, disguised as other merchandise, when needed for the pleasure of the establishment's customers. Cash on delivery was the usual method of payment. Only the biggest of buyers, well established as reputable, would be allowed a latter payment. No one ever paid ahead of time. It was a simple business, involving very few risks. Occasionally, a speeding driver, careless or sleepy would roll his car on some remote gravel road, smash the merchandise, suffering the loss of his shipment, and the expense of repairing his auto. One other slight risk was the occasional mayor or sheriff running on reform ticket, getting elected, then having to prove his threat's by raiding a contact man's garage full of booze or a rural dance hall full of people who voted against him in the election. If he dared anything further than confiscating the liquor that was out in the open, he found himself in dire danger of his family being threatened or a rock-born note being thrown through his window. Sig's men and their customers did not take these interruptions kindly. A newly elected sheriff, Stan Mikorsky, in Becker County, Minnesota, east of Fargo, North Dakota became very brazen. He turned down the bribes his predecessor had received from the owners of two dance halls. Then he raided the two dance halls, both on Saturday nights when they were jammed with patrons, broke into their back rooms, smashed all of liquor bottles, emptied the dance halls, put the owners in hand cuffs and nailed the doors shut. Several weeks later, puffed up from his dance hall success, he busted into a pool hall in Detroit Lakes, smashed down the door to the back room and smashed all of the liquor bottles there. This was after he had been entertained the previous week, in Minneapolis, by the owner of the pool hall where the sheriff and his wife were feted to a dinner at Charlie's Café', a night baseball game of the Saint Paul Saints against the Minneapolis Millers, and a night at the Nicolett Hotel. A month later, on a Thursday night, out of his uniform, his custom once a month, he attended the Deep Fried Gizzard Night at the American Legion Hall in his hometown of White Earth. It was an all men affair with tables of various card games after the supper.

Tables for five card stud poker were in the back room, itself illegal in Becker County, but enjoyed by Sheriff Mikorsky. He was a double dealer, no illegal liquor for the common folks but illegal poker for himself. Late that night he pulled into the driveway of his home, his house dark, Mrs. Mikorsky having long been in bed. When he got out of his car, two hooded men stepped from behind two large elm trees alongside his drive. One of the men placed a strangle hold on the sheriff before he could utter a sound. The other hooded man placed a pistol with a silencer against the back of the sheriff's head. One shot and he slumped to the ground. The man with the gun shot four more bullets into the sheriff's chest. The two men then walked quickly to a big black car as it drove up, without its lights on, not even coming to a complete stop as the men jumped in. Mrs. Mikorsky never even woke up. Her husband had the habit of often staying out all night. The next morning, the milkman found the sheriff's body. The murder was big news locally and regionally, no one daring to suggest that it could have been a deal from the underworld. No one wanted to be next. A special election took place to replace the sheriff. No reformist ran for office. A man, who could look the other way, if his palm was greased, won the election. The murder was investigated very superficially. What was there to investigate? No arrests were made.

The Clutch Shop was busy beyond belief. Clutch had another building erected on the back of his property for a body shop. His customers were not only occasionally rolling in their autos, but were smashing their fenders and headlights at intersections and backing into trees. He saw a chance to reap more profit. He was paying off his original loan from Sig so fast it was hard to believe. Now with the body shop in business his position had become more and more managerial. He had his own desk in the front office. A second office girl was hired. The total work force, including him, was now ten. It wasn't only Sig's gang that was keeping the shop humming. They were becoming a smaller and smaller part of the total business. The census of automobiles on the street was increasing tremendously. Soon, nearly every family had an auto.

Sig invited Clutch to a weekend at his home on Lake Geneva. It was all fun and leisure all day Saturday, horseback riding, swimming, an hour at the billiard table and a speedboat ride on the lake. Saturday evening, Sig divulged the reason for the invitation. He invited Clutch to become a major person in his business. Clutch's talents were well recognized by Sig. He wanted to make use of them. Sig's point man in the immediate vicinity of Janesville was being transferred to Northern Minnesota. The market for liquor in Minnesota was no longer just Minneapolis, Saint Paul, and Saint Cloud. It was expanding to the booming resort area in Northern Minnesota. Would Clutch oversee the Janesville area? The remuneration would be in excess of what he was now taking in. His total income would be more that twice what he was making now. Clutch said, "Don Sigarto Bellagio, I will have to think about your generous offer. It is very attractive." "You will not have to give up your shop, Clutch." There was no more discussion. The two men each had a glass of Gilliano Liquor and went back to the billiard table. Sunday morning, after a swim in the pool with Sig and his family, the two men played tennis. Sig had a mean serve and was swift on his feet. Clutch had very little experience in the game, only a few matches when he was staying at the YMCA. It was no match. Clutch gave his answer to Sig that Monday. "Yes!"

CHAPTER FOUR

Clutch bought another new Austin/Healey, the best on the road, particularly after he had it supercharged in his shop. He kept it polished spotless, frequently greased, not a squeak in it. About the same time, Clutch had become acquainted with a young lady who had brought her father's car to his shop for some extensive work. She was in Clutch's office several times. He found her very attractive, her name Josephine Peterson, of the Swedish descent. He invited her out to dinner and a movie for an evening. She was indeed impressed with his auto. Josephine's folks were impressed with Clutch. Her father had a large jewelry store in Janesville, obviously successful. The family home was very impressive, twelve foot ceilings, imported chandeliers, Turkish carpeting throughout, two servants with their own quarters over the garage. Clutch was invited to the home several times for Sunday dinners, after which he and the Petersons played hearts in the card room. Later in the day Clutch and Josephine would take a ride into the country in Clutch's Austin/Healy. As dusk approached, Clutch would stop on some hidden country lane. The two would talk and spoon with proper amour. They talked of marriage. One Saturday, Clutch bought a beautiful one-caret diamond ring, which he brought with him on Sunday. Late that afternoon, Clutch proposed. Josephine gasped at the size of the ring. She accepted. They went immediately to Josephine's parents, who gave their consent. No precise date for the wedding was set.

Josephine had not previously inquired deeply into Clutch's past family life, nor his present business activities, until one evening about one month after their engagement she put out some feelers. Her folks had been asking her some questions she had not been able to answer. Clutch told her of his long separation from his family for five years. He led Josephine to believe he was soon going back to North Dakota to make a visit. She was satisfied with that. She did not ask too much about his current business, assuming his sole enterprise was **THE CLUTCH SHOP.** It was only when they started to go out more on Saturday nights to dinner and the movies, following which they would often visit Clutch's favorite speakeasy in the hilly farm country east of Janesville, then she raised some more questions. The speakeasy was disguised as a farm place with all of the necessary buildings and activities, farm livestock, etc. The only unlikeness to a regular farm was that there were two big barns on the place; one the regular barn with dairy cows, work horses, calves, sheep, cats, errant chickens; the other barn secluded by trees, with all of the outside appearances of a regular farm barn, but with a large parking lot adjacent to the barn, also secluded by trees and several knolls in the terrain. Only when one entered the barn did one see the difference; false windows so no inside light could escape as a giveaway, finished off with interior knotty pine walls, several stand-up bars, fancy booths, ornate chandeliers and a stage on one end with a dance band playing the latest, including the current Charleston numbers and with a small sunken dance floor. Josephine loved to go there with Clutch; they would dance to the wee hours. It was at this speakeasy that Josephine formed some questions. There would always be a group of surly men at the bar who never failed to greet Clutch. They often had girlfriends with them. At times they mentioned to Clutch they wanted to talk to him. Clutch would leave Josephine in the booth often for extended periods. This would bother Josephine. She demanded to know why these surly men were more important to Clutch than she was. Clutch begged the question by saying they were customers at his shop and were just trying to get some free advice out of him about their automobiles. He would say, "Josephine, I do not want to be rude to them. They are good customers." Josephine accepted Clutch's explanation.

That fall, Clutch obtained a different apartment, more luxurious, furnished, underground garage for his Austin/Healy. A cleaning lady every day did his laundry, washed the dirty dishes, made his bed, kept the place spotless for him. Josephine acquired a desire to spend quite a bit of time there herself, mostly evenings when she expected Clutch to be home. He had given her a key. She would sometimes arrive early and prepare the evening meal for both of them. Sometimes he would call her from the shop and tell her he wanted to go out and eat, usually at a late hour. She never called him at the shop, but one evening he was not at his apartment when she expected and he had not telephoned her to discuss his plans. She rang up the shop. One of the bookkeepers was still there. Josephine said, "Is Clutch there?" The answer, "No, he hasn't been here all afternoon." Josephine wondered! Clutch did not roll into the apartment until near midnight. Josephine had waited. Clutch found her crying. She could tell that Clutch had been drinking some. She sobbed, "Where have you been, darling?" Clutch had a guilty, trapped feeling. He knew he could not avoid an answer. He said, "Josie, (a nickname he seldom used, only when trying to gain favor), I have never told you before, but I have another business besides the shop. It takes me away from the shop at times." Josephine sniffled, "Can you tell me what the business is?" "Of course, I can. It is a delivery business." Then he said quickly, "Lets go out for a midnight snack." He grabbed Josephine's arm and out the door they went. Josephine stayed with Clutch in his apartment that night. She had been doing this quite often. Their love was complete. They employed rhythm and hygienic measures to prevent pregnancy, but were prepared to marry quickly if Josephine had become pregnant. Her folks knew of their daughter's fulfilled love. Josephine had told her mother of her passion for Clutch and how he had relished sleeping with her. Her folks had no choice but to accept the arrangement. After all, they did admire Clutch, his friendly personality, his business accomplishment, and his kindness to their daughter. The only thing left was to set a wedding date, which the couple said would probably not be until next spring.

Clutch's area of operation under Don Sigarto Bellagio's Mafiosa was relatively free of troubles. The boundaries were quite sharply defined; the Illinois border to the south, the Iowa border to the west, and a line straight north from Janesville defining the east border and a line straight east from La Crosse defining the north border. Basically this encompassed the southwest corner of the State of Wisconsin. The operation was limited to the provision of bootlegged whiskey to speakeasies, pool halls, and dance halls. It had been learned from experience that to store large supplies in warehouses was unsafe. The Feds or some lesser law enforcement agency would some way or other find out about the location and the entire stock would be lost in a raid. Best that bootlegged whiskey be kept on the move, as its name implied, offered for sale out of the upper part of the leg of a boot. Disguised as it was in ocean going vessels from Europe to New Orleans, it was moved to Mississippi River Cargo ships, bypassing any warehouse. Likewise in Chicago, it was taken off the riverboats and immediately hauled away in the high-speed autos of Sig's gang, directly to the destination points. Shipments destined for the rest of Wisconsin, the states of Minnesota and the Dakota's, passed through Milwaukee mostly via railroad baggage cars and finally automobiles. Clutch's men never let their merchandise out of their sight from the time they picked it up in Chicago until it was delivered. If the drivers needed sleep or it was the wrong time of the day to make the delivery, they slept in their cars with the booze. If some reform law officer was waiting in hiding in hopes of making an arrest at the time of delivery of the booze, he wouldn't find his mission that easy to accomplish. The bootlegger would seldom give up without a fight. A gun battle would ensue, usually with the law officer being the loser, injured or sometimes dead. If a car chase took place, seldom would the bootlegger lose the race. His car would be faster and would be better armored. The law officer would be left in a cloud of dust.

One night Clutch accompanied the delivery person. He wanted to visit with the Sugar River Dance Hall operator who had become behind in his payments to the Bellagio Liquor Syndicate. There had been a rendevous point pre-established on a wooded side road near the town of Attica. Somehow, the local sheriff had been tipped off. He set up an ambush by himself and two temporary deputies he had sworn in that afternoon in his office in Monroe, the county seat of Green County in which Attica was located. The two were inexperienced and the sheriff himself not too bright. The rendezvous point was an old abandoned barn about 50 yards off the side road. As Clutch's and his associates car had just barely pulled off the road, the two inexperienced deputies panicked, turned on a big search light that illuminated the sheriff, standing by a tree, more than it did Clutch's car. The two temporary deputies immediately fired their guns, 38 cal. Pistols at Clutch's car and not too accurately. Clutch returned the fire, out his window on the right hand side of the car, with a Thomas sub-machine gun he had been holding in his lap. Both deputies slumped to the ground riddled from head to foot. The sheriff, by now hidden behind the tree, never fired his gun. The operator of the dance hall, now lying on the floor of the barn with his hands covering his head was hollering, "I give up! I give up!" Not a word of it audible above the musical notes of Clutch's machine gun. Even before Clutch was done firing, his driver had turned their auto back onto the road, and with stones flying off his spinning wheels was headed out of there. The driver saw in his rear view mirror what he assumed was the sheriff's car pulling out on the road and heading the other way. It wasn't until they were down the road a ways that Clutch felt something wet running down his left arm. He put his right hand under his jacket and found it was blood flowing briskly from his shoulder area. He had noted no pain there in the excitement of the shoot out. Clutch applied pressure on the wound with a clean white handkerchief, while the driver drove speedily to the Janesville Hospital emergency room a good 25 miles away, at times revving his Italian Lancia up over 100 miles per hour. A surgeon took Clutch to the operating room shortly after reaching the hospital. The bullet was easily removed, not too deep, and it had only fractured the tip of the clavicle. The wound was not closed tight but left open with a drain in place to reduce the chance of infection. Clutch knew Josephine was at her parent's home so he did not contact her that night. What was he going to tell her? The question was on his subconscious mind in the dark of the night. He decided to tell her the truth. Clutch had a nurse telephone Josephine the next morning to tell her he was in the hospital. She was at the hospital by 10:00 that morning. She cried real tears when she saw Clutch in the white bed all bandaged up. She cried, "What has happened to you?" Clutch responded, "Oh Nothing! I was shot in the shoulder. It isn't bad." She blurted out, "You were shot? By whom?" "A sheriff, He replied calmly. He was slow to get the story out. Josephine's patience and anxiety were wearing thin. She demanded firmly, "Tell me the whole thing." He did, confessing his second job away from the shop was as a manager of a group of bootleggers and that he and one of his underlings were caught in an ambush, where there was an exchange of gunfire, one bullet striking him in the shoulder. It was a glancing shot off the doorframe of the car, so did little damage to him and the bullet had already been removed. Josephine now had two concerns; Clutch's health, and his confession of his second life, in the underworld. The second concern was not entirely a surprise. She had some previous suspicions. Now it was out in the open. Josephine cried uncontrollably for a long time, her head on Clutch's bed, right arm wrapped around her. She stayed by Clutch's bedside till after he had been served his lunch, He ate little from his tray. There was next to no more conversation. Clutch was kept at rest for an entire week. Josephine visited him at least twice every day, always embracing and kissing him on arrival and departure. Their love had not been weakened by Clutch's disclosure. Josephine had given her folks a story, saying Clutch had been in an automobile accident. They had visited Clutch several times. He supported Josephine's story to her folks. The newspaper stories of the deputies' deaths made front-page headlines, but there was no suggestion of who may have been the gunmen. Readers were led to believe it was all a mystery to the sheriff. He vowed to solve the case, but in the best interests of doing so, had to refuse giving out details. The truth was, he feared for his own life if he talked too much. It further came out in the newspaper that the Sugar River Dance Hall operator was deeply in debt to others than the Bellagio Liquor Syndicate, the latter, of course not being mentioned in the newspaper. Don Sigarto Bellagio had met with the editors of the local newspapers to take care of that by passing a goodly sum of cash and a few firm innuendos. The editors understood. It subsequently came out in the newspapers that the Sugar River Dance Hall operator lost the dance hall to his creditors. Don Sigarto Bellagio did not visit Clutch in the hospital but passed word through one of his other captains who he had to visit Clutch, that he offered his sympathies and also had the captain suggest that it be best that Clutch not discuss the incident with anyone and that the operator of the Sugar River Dance Hall would offer retribution for his unpaid debt with the Bellagio Liquor Syndicate. Shortly after, headlines in the JANESVILLE MORNING TIMES read: **"Dance Hall Operator Murdered"**. His body had been found bloated and floating in the Sugar River. The event resulted in reducing the number of unpaid debts to Bellagio to zero for years to come.

Following his hospitalization, Clutch had to visit his surgeon's office daily to have his wound re packed. The surgeon was insistent on the wound healing from the bottom out, not being able to heal over on top, leaving a pocket deep in the wound. The surgeon had been a US Army surgeon in World War I. He knew from experience that bullet wounds could not be closed primarily. Infection in the wound, sepsis, and subsequent septicemia, and death would be the consequence. The only initial treatment in the operating room, the night Clutch was shot, was thorough cleansing of the wound, ligation of the bleeding vessels and packing. The method left an ugly scar but saved Clutch's life. The surgeon ordered Clutch to not do any shop work until the wound was completely closed. That was over a month. His time at the shop had been mostly managerial for some time anyway, so that was really no big problem to him.

Josephine was skirmishing with herself every day over her discovery of Clutch's second life in the underworld. She both did and did not want to share the matter with someone. She had no real close girl friends, no one she really chummed with. Her life, for sometime, had been devoted to Clutch, full time. The minister at her church did not seem the type to accept such puzzlement. Her family's doctor was certainly not a confidant. Who else was there? No one. She brought up the matter with Clutch many times. He was reluctant to accept her disbelief. He saw nothing wrong with being a bootlegger. He had more trouble explaining the murders, except to say, "They had it coming." Josephine came right out and asked Clutch to quit the bootlegging job, and just stick to THE CLUTCH SHOP. "Please, Clutch, I love you so much. I cannot stand to see you going against the law. You will get hurt or killed." Clutch would not promise. All he would say was, "Maybe." Josephine decided to talk to her folks. They were aghast, horror struck when they heard of the story. At first they were grievous, then became loathsome. They were adamant that Clutch had to change his life. Josephine's dad would talk to Clutch. Josephine wasn't sure that was going to be the best thing to do. He went right to Clutch's shop, found him in his office, asked in, then shut the door. He announced immediately what Josephine had told him and Josephine's mother. Clutch did not bat an eye. Josephine's father made it very clear that he was withdrawing permission for Clutch to marry his daughter if Clutch would not sever his connections to the underworld. Clutch showed that he really did not appreciate Josephine's father busting in on him to make such straight demands. He said, "I'll think about it." Then Clutch showed Josephine's father the door. Clutch was stubborn. His life from childhood reflected his rebelliousness. No one had ever been able to tell him what to do. He knew, from the second Josephine's father had entered his office; his engagement with Josephine was off. No one was going to make demands of him. If he met Josephine's demands this time, it would not be the last demand by Josephine and her parents he would have to meet. He would not have a wife who was not a partner in his life as well as his partner in bed.

Josephine came over to Clutch's apartment that evening. Her father had told her of his visit with Clutch. She begged with sobbing pleas for Clutch to give in, reiterating over and over her love for him. He would not give in. He said, "Our engagement is off."

Josephine left in tears, then, in a second, came back, taking off her engagement ring and putting it in Clutch's hand. They never saw each other again. Josephine's folks sent her off that fall to Smith College, an all girls' school in Northampton, Massachusetts.

CHAPTER FIVE

THE CLUTCH SHOP continued to do well financially. The bootlegging of liquor also was a booming business. Americans were taking too social drinking more and more. Law enforcement authorities were finding it increasingly more and more difficult to suppress the trade. Clutch and his underlings had very few episodes of difficulty in their district. Establishments asking for delivery of the Bellagio's Syndicate's product paid on delivery. Law officers took "hush money" and looked the other way. Businesses serving liquor kept their own law and order. They had henchman to take care of troublemakers. Bouncers at the pool halls, speakeasies and dance halls bounced drunks without hesitation, even taking them to their homes if they were unfit to drive their cars, thus avoiding accidents that could reflect on the establishments. If the disciplined customers or their families tried in any way to create adverse publicity for the establishments, they would likely receive a personal visit from a representative of the liquor-selling establishment involved. A modest payment would be offered. In return the party would be asked to discuss the matter in public no more and to not visit the establishment again. If the party refused the offer or in any way violated the agreement in the future, the matter would be turned over to the Bellagio Syndicate deliveryman. He in turn wound turn it over to his captain. In Clutch's district he handled these matters directly, unless they were in or close to Janesville, where he might be known or recognized. In that case he would ask for help from Don Sigarto Bellagio. The Don would likely assign the matter to one of his lieutenants. Clutch had one such troublesome case in his district late that summer. A big pool hall in the Mississippi River city of Prairie du Chein, Wisconsin that had a locked door lounge in the back of the building was being tormented by a customer who had been bounced one night for drunkenness. He was literally thrown out the back door, without being offered a ride home. His behavior had also been undesirable previously. He was a low-grade politician of sorts with a reputation for causing trouble. He tried to gain entrance to the lounge again about a week hence. He was refused. The proprietor had permanently black listed him. Being a blowhard, he was offended, and visited a shyster lawyer in the nearby city of Boscobel, 25 miles northeast of Prairie du Chein. The lawyer wrote the proprietor of the pool hall threatening to sue the pool hall if his client was not paid a huge reward. The pool hall proprietor told his Bellagio deliveryman about the threat, who in turn told Clutch. A few inquires disclosed the lawyer visited his favorite speakeasy in Boscobel every evening before driving home. This time of the year it would be dark by the time he would be expected to drive up his driveway. He was not in the habit of driving his car into his garage. The next Thursday afternoon Clutch, and two of the Don's henchmen, drove to Boscobel, arriving some before sunset, cased the area around the lawyer's home, parked their car on a side street around the corner from the lawyer's home, covered the license plates on their car and secluded themselves behind a row of bushes along the lawyer's driveway. All was quiet in the neighborhood, only an occasional auto driving down the street, no loose dogs, only one tied up critter offering an infrequent yelp. Clutch and his men did not have to wait long. The car stopped in the driveway as predicted. The lawyer stepped out. The one henchman was behind him in a flash, thong around the lawyer's neck, preventing him from uttering a sound, then falling to the ground unconscious. Clutch and his men, all three, had on black hoods. In the meantime Clutch ran to his car, drove it up on the lawn where the two henchmen threw the body of the lawyer on the back floor and climbed on top of him. Clutch sped off, not stopping until they reached a dark wooded lane, Clutch had earlier in the evening identified as a good spot to work over the lawyer. There they stopped and allowed the lawyer to come to his senses. Clutch mixed no words about the mission's intentions. "Leave the pool hall operator in Prairie du Chein alone. Do you understand?" The lawyer answered, with a hoarse tremble in his voice, "Yes, I do." With that response, Clutch ordered his two henchmen to throw the man out. Clutch sped off, leaving the lawyer in the woods, 10 miles from his home, in the dark of night. He was disoriented, not knowing where he was, or what the directions were. It was cloudy, beginning to rain, no moon or stars. He walked down the little used woodland trail in the direction Clutch's car had driven, coming to a dirt country road. He again turned left. A car passed. He hailed it. The lawyer offered the driver a buck to take him to his home in Boscobel. As he busted in the front door, his wife hollered, "Where have you been?" She had not even noticed his car in the driveway. Then she saw, he was all roughed up, his clothes torn, wet and muddy, so his story was believable. Then the lawyer telephoned the sheriff of Grant County in Lancaster. He denied jurisdiction, asking the lawyer if his home wasn't north of the Wisconsin River on the edge of Boscobel, telling him that it was in Crawford County. The lawyer accused the sheriff of giving him the run around. He telephoned the sheriff of Crawford County in Prairie du Chein. He acted disinterested but offered to send his deputy to Boscobel to investigate. The deputy arrived at the lawyer's home near midnight, asked a few questions, looked for car tracks on the lawn, and said he could see nothing, promised to visit the woodland spot where the lawyer was thrown out of the car, saying he knew where it was. The site was never visited. The case was closed. The sheriff and his deputy had previously had a meeting with Clutch in the parking lot of the Prairie du Chien pool hall. Their palms, at that time, were well greased by a substantial amount of cold, hard cash.

The lawyer was not an easy learner. He wrote another letter to the pool hall operator making worse threats than in the first letter. He also started carrying a 45-caliber revolver in a shoulder holster. He had fired it several times along the river, that being the limit of his practice with it. One week later, the lawyer was again late for supper. In the dark of the night, his wife opened the front door, saw his auto in the driveway, went outside, and walked around the car where she saw her husband laying on the ground, a pool of blood beside his head. His revolver was on the ground beside him. She ran back inside the house, screaming, "They have killed him." She then fainted onto the living room couch. Her oldest son took a look at what his mother had seen then telephoned the city cop. He was without an automobile, had to walk from downtown Boscobel. It was a while before he arrived at the lawyer's house. In the meantime word spread around the neighborhood. When the cop arrived, the yard was full of people, some very concerned about violent crime in their neighborhood. The street was full of cars. Someone had picked up the revolver and thrown a blanket over the body. The cop asked for the revolver. On examining it he noticed the cylinder was full. He turned the body over, finding a bullet hole in the back of the skull and several more in the chest. "Murder! He telephoned the sheriff's office in Prairie du Chien. The same deputy that had been to the lawyer's house previously answered the phone. He said he would be there promptly. He arrived several hours later. After looking over the body and the murder site he called the undertaker. Case closed!

CHAPTER SIX

About this time Clutch spent a weekend at Don Sigarto Bellagio's home on Lake Geneva. The Don had just returned from his annual visit to Sicily. The Don and Clutch discussed Clutch's work. The Don complimented Clutch. Clutch asked the Don if he could take a vacation, visit his family in Voltaire, North Dakota. The Don thought Clutch's request was very reasonable. He would select someone to substitute in his position as captain of the Janesville district during Clutch's absence. "How long do you want to be gone?" he asked Clutch. "About a month, if that is okay?" responded Clutch. "Fine with me. When do you want to leave?" said the Don. "September 1st, said Clutch. "Fine, I'll plan on your return October 1st," responded the Don. The Don and Clutch played a lot of pool that weekend. Clutch had been spending more time in his favorite Janesville pool hall since his break up with Josephine. The practice showed. He beat the Don nearly every game. The tennis court was another matter. There the Don still held supreme.

Clutch sent his sister, Priscella, a telegram, PLAN TO VISIT YOU AND THE FAMILY WILL DRIVE MY CAR, PLANNING TO ARRIVE ABOUT SEPTEMBER 4TH. LOVE, JIM. The Doyer's had a phone but the depot agent could not get them to answer, so he brought the telegram to the post office. It was delivered the next day to the mailbox at the old Morgan place where Priscella now lived. She and the son of the new family living there had been married in July so she moved in with his family. Her name was now Mrs. Sven Peterson. She had not written Jim since this recent happening. It was now too close to Jim's departure date to write him. Jim would have to wait to find out about her marriage when he arrived at their folks place. The Peterson's and the Doyers had rural phones installed recently. Priscella immediately rang her stepmother, Ann, 2 longs, 2 shorts! Ann answered the phone. Priscella said, delightedly, "Jim's coming home, in just a couple of days. I just received a Western Union Telegram. I'd run it over but Sven's dad is gone with the truck. Is your truck home?" Both families had acquired second hand trucks recently, Model-T Fords with home made boxes on the back. Farm prices were good. Ann responded, excitedly, "Ours is here I'll be right over." Lee was in the field, picking corn. Shane was not home, working out with a farmer helping harvest. Jeanie had also been out working all summer, helping a nearby farm wife. Winston, Mary, Amy, Kim and Helen were out in the garden picking tomatoes and digging potatoes. Ann turned into Peterson's lane so fast the old Model-T truck went up on two wheels nearly rolling over. It was a hot, windless day. Dust hung over Ann's route down the township road, and over Peterson's lane in a timeless cloud, an ethereal omen of good times to come.

The two women gaggled incessantly, the children attempting to interrupt with questions and pulling of skirts. They planned dinner parties, pheasant and sharp tailed grouse hunt with the men, barn dances, and church socials, all without much consideration for what Jim's tastes would be. Jim's arrival date was but one week away. Both the ladies had a lot of garden canning to do before Jim's arrival. Neither knew if he was married, probably not, or even if he was engaged. He had made no mention of bringing anybody with him. His life was a mystery. Ann stayed at Peterson's place till late afternoon. When she reached home she drove right to the field where Lee was picking corn. She could not wait to tell him the news. He reacted with more animation than she had. It was a psychological moment for Lee. The days and years of Jim's being gone, the not knowing, then the news on the post card. He shut his eyes. The entire story shone brilliantly in front of him, as though it was being shown on a movie screen. He stood there with his eyes shut for the longest time, Ann and the children quiet, with the heads bowed in reverence. Lee broke the silence, "I can't stay out here in this field alone and its nearly quitting time anyway, you all get back to the house. I'm driving this load of corn in. As soon as I've unloaded it and unharnessed, watered and fed the horses, I'll be in the house. They all sat and talked at the kitchen table for a good hour. Lee asked over and over about the details of the telegram, asked of Priscella and Ann's plans, questioning the wisdom of some of them. He preferred the alternative of not making too many plans till Jim was present to state his preferences. He was a little late that evening getting to his barn chores of milking, hog slopping, currying and feeding the horses, feeding the chickens and ducks, gathering eggs and hand pumping water into the stock tank. There had been no wind for three days to turn the windmill. Winston pitched in to help, which was his usual responsibility.

After chores it was supper, dark by that time. The entire family, including Priscella's Sven, sat down to the table for grace, led by Lee. He was quite emotional particularly in thanking the Lord for Jim's upcoming return. The table was full of wholesome victuals; cold fried chicken left from noon dinner, potato salad, fried tomatoes, hot sliced garden beets, floating in melted butter, choice of lemonade, whole milk or coffee for a beverage, ground cherry sauce and gingersnap cookies for dessert. Talk about Jim's coming continued way past when the dishes were washed. The Coleman gas lamp over the table illuminated the entire kitchen. It had been too hot to fire up the kitchen range. Cooking had been done on a kerosene stove located in the back room, attached to the house. The gas engine operated washing machine was also located in the back room. In the rafters of the room hung the last two of the previous winter's smoked hams and several slabs of cured bacon. Maggots had gotten into one of the hams in the middle of the summer, requiring Ann to get it down and trim out the bad spot, where apparently brine had not penetrated deeply, attracting flies to lay a few eggs. The ham suffered little damage. Nobody went to bed early, even the small children, Amy now age 11, Kim, now age 10 and Helen, now age 9, were allowed to stay up. They were mystified by the talk of this brother, Jim, having been too young when he left to be able to remember him clearly. Even Winston, age 10 when Jim left, now age 15, was having trouble developing a clear picture of his long absent brother. The telegram had arrived on Thursday, August 31st. Priscella figured Jim was going to leave Janesville on Saturday morning. He should arrive in Voltaire late Monday or if he stopped any time in Minneapolis it could push his arrival ahead to Tuesday.

Clutch had a fair amount of details to attend to the week he was to leave. He had a good foreman at the shop but there were a few things he did not know about the way Clutch handled matters, particularly with the cars owned by the delivery men of the Bellagio Syndicate. He made it very clear to the foreman that "Omerta", the Mafia code of silence, was an inviolable rule. Violation of "Omerta" could lead to the penalty of death. He told the foreman, "Talk to no one. If someone asks questions, do not answer them." Clutch took his replacement around to introduce him to the customers. That took three days. The list was long. Clutch had his Austin/Healy thoroughly serviced. He packed six of his best suits. He visited the barbershop for a haircut and a manicure. A case of the best French Brandy was stashed in the trunk of the car. The morning he left he sprayed himself with cologne of the most tantalizing aroma. The highway to Minneapolis had been surfaced with concrete just the previous summer. From Minneapolis to Valley City it was going to be patchy. From Valley City to Voltaire it was going to be dusty gravel. His thoughts were deep that morning of departure from Janesville. He had feelings of satisfaction with his accomplishments. He here was not even 21 years of age. Not until November of this year of 1927 would he hit that mark. He had recently become nostalgic about his home, his family, even feeling a little guilty for what he had done to them five years ago. These deep thoughts hung on his mind that morning. The travel that day was without problems. Many travelers were encumbered with tire trouble. Not Clutch, he had recently replaced his tires with the best, imported from France. He sailed along smoothly, stopping only for a quick lunch at a café on the main street of La Crosse, and filling his gas tank as needed at roadside filling stations. He reached downtown Minneapolis in time for dinner at the Curtis Hotel and then to bed. He was up for an early breakfast and then was back on the highway. Travel was not as smooth that day, speed according to the patchiness of surfaced highway. He arrived in Valley City near midnight, checked into the Valley City hotel and telephoned Joe and Trudy the next morning. They were ecstatic, invited Clutch to come out for breakfast. When he drove up proudly in his Austin/Healey, the whole family was in the yard to greet him. Trudy and the kids hugged him lovingly. Joe gave him a bear hug. They had many questions. Clutch had many tales to tell. He suppressed any talk about his job with Don Sigarto Bellagio. Joe didn't go to work until Clutch left about 10:00. Clutch had put on his Harris Tweed topcoat and brown derby in the morning. It was early fall, cool in North Dakota, different than southern Wisconsin. Trudy had commented on how dapper he looked, told him to beware or some North Dakota vixen would latch on to him. He slipped Joe a bottle of brandy as they parted. Clutch stopped briefly at the old shop to greet Sparky. He found him prosperous and happy. The highway west of Valley City to Jamestown was paved concrete. North out of Jamestown to Carrington it was good gravel but from Carrington, west and then north to Fessenden it was rutted, slow going, shaking the heck out of the Austin/Healy. It continued poor through Harvey, all the way to Voltaire. It was late afternoon when he headed straight south out of Voltaire to his folks place. He drove slow to be able to clarify his remembrances, scanning the horizon for old landmarks. Many of the building sites looked unfamiliar. Tractors were working many more fields than at the time he had left. In just five years there were many new barns, some new houses. There were even a few automobiles on the road, occupants waving to Jim as though they knew him. Of course, the entire community knew he was coming to visit his family. After all these years of absence, this was novel news, worth spreading. Even the VELVA WEEKLY GAZETTE reporter had driven out to Doyer's place that morning to get the story for publication in the upcoming issue, due out Friday. The Velva paper was the only publication between Harvey and Minot. Those last five miles of his trip were heavy with nostalgia. He had been an angry young man to crawl out of bed that night, sneak out of the house and hike to Bergen. How would his father react to his returning now, after five years? He would soon find out. As he turned off the road into the farm lane he slowed to a stop, only then noticing five children lying in a barrow ditch. They had been there half the afternoon waiting for Jim wanting to be the first to see him. When Jim's auto stopped they jumped up and ran to it, jumping on the running board, their dog, Bum right with them. Jim yelled, "Jump in." Winston said, "We can run to the house." Jim responded, "Get in. I want to take you for a spin." Winston and Mary climbed into the front seat. Amy, Kim and Helen in the back. Jim backed out onto the road and headed towards the next corner in a swirl of dust, Bum barking behind, trying to keep up. Jim swerved the car in the loose dirt, further delighting the children. The window's including the windshield were all wide open, wind blowing through Jim's and the children's hair. Jim wheeled the car in a spin at the corner. The kids shrieked with delight. Back at the lane, Jim slowed down to a crawl, than gassed the engine to full throttle till the auto was even with the porch where he cut the ignition, jumped out while the auto was still rolling and jumped up on the porch. The group had observed the entire escapade with the children, amused but impatient to greet Jim. He had discarded his Harris Tweed, brown derby and suit coat earlier, now in his shirt- sleeves, with flowered elastic armbands on both arms. He was happy with himself, feeling bold and excited, grabbing Priscella first, hugging her till she could hardly breathe, kissing her with wet lips on both cheeks, her mouth, her bust and both arms. She had on a tight low-necked sleeveless blouse. Jim said, "Priscella, you look so beautiful." Ann received the next hug and kiss with a thank you, "Ann, thanks so much for taking such good care of my dad and my sisters and brothers." To Shane he said, "My you are a big man," as he gave him a bear hug. Jeanie, being at a shy age was hanging back. Jim reached back behind Ann, pulling Jeanie forward, as he said." You are my little sweetie." Then he gave her a big buzz on the lips. Dad was grinning from ear to ear. Jim grabbed his Dads hands as he said, "Dad, you will never know how I have missed you." Lee said, "You'll never know how glad I am to see you Jim." With that they both put their arms around each other with tears in their eyes and no more words. Ann said, "O! Come on you two cry babies, let's all go inside and have some lemonade and cookies." Everyone headed for the kitchen, where they all pulled up chairs to the huge table. First questions first; what is your work, Jim? Are you married? No. Do you have a girlfriend? Do you own the car you came in? Are you going back to Wisconsin? How long are you going to stay? Where do you live in Janesville, a house, an apartment, a rooming house, a hotel, with a friend? His answers were vague. He planned on staying about a month. He wanted no one to arrange his time, nothing at the church. He wanted to just be a plain farm boy. Lee said, "It sounds good to me. Now I've got to do chores. I am already late." Jim responded, "I'll help. Have you an extra pair of coveralls and barn boots? Ann butted in, "You don't have to help." Jim rebutted rather cocky, "Well I am going to. What do you think I am here for, to sit on my duff?" Jim found a pair of coveralls hanging in the back shed off the kitchen, and a pair of rubber Wellingtons standing by the back door. "You kids gather the hen eggs and feed the chickens and ducks and then help your mother get what she needs from the garden or whatever.

Lee and Jim walked past the windmill on the way to the barn. A breeze had been blowing all afternoon. The stock tank was full of water. The water was running through the cream cooler fresh and swift. The cows had been up from the pasture for a good hour, wanting to be milked. The horses were standing by the gate hoping they would be put in their stalls for a feeding of oats. Lee ignored them. They hadn't worked all afternoon, didn't deserve grain. Only one horse was kept in the barn. The rest could go to pasture if they were still hungry. In the barn, Jim grabbed a milk pail and milk stool and went to the cow in the second stanchion. As he looked her over carefully, he exclaimed, "Sadie, are you still giving milk?" She had been a fresh heifer with calf when Jim had left five years previously. Lee said, "Jim, she has been my best producer, a calf every year, twins one year." Jim sat on his stool alongside Sadie. She turned her head to look at him, realizing he was a stranger, but then nodded acceptance. Jim was slow at getting his hands to pull effectively on the teats. It had been five years. Lee had finished two cows before Jim was through with Sadie, but Jim had filled two pails and stripped Sadie dry. There were twelve cows to milk but the time passed quickly with the two men chatting like a couple of hens the whole time. Little of the talk was about when Jim ran away. That was over the dam, to be forgotten. Jim's favorite topic was his dad's situation on the farm. It was apparent that conditions were better than when Jim had left; a telephone, a truck, the children well dressed, a new hog shed, new cream separator, the farm place generally in good repair, all signs of moderate farm affluence. Jim complimented his dad on his progress. At the same time, Jim was aware of the financial moderation that ruled that family's life. He dwelt on his thoughts. Maybe there was something he could do while he was home that would improve life for his family, relieve the heavy burden of farm life, just a little bit. The milk was separated when the milking was over with. The DeVaul separator was hand crank operated. Jim started revving up the separator while Lee finished the last cow. The cream ran into a five-gallon can while the milk ran into a pail, which was dumped into a slop drum every time it filled up. The slop drum was on a stone sled, for pulling it to the hog shed. The mixture of ground grain and skim milk was poured into the hog troughs with a big rusty pail, accompanied by much squealing and shoving by the hogs. They relished this twice a day delight. Lee did too. Every pound on their carcasses was dollars in the bank. The hog market was good. It was 8:00 when they went to the house, carrying all the milking equipment with them to be thoroughly washed by Ann.

Supper was baked ham and sweet potatoes, other garden produce, fresh bread, apple-pie with cheese, milk, lemonade and coffee. The ham had been glazed with honey/apple preserve. Sven, Priscella's husband, had come over for supper to meet Jim. There was little conversation. Everyone was dead tired. Jim asked Lee what he was going to do the next day. Lee said, "Pick corn." Jim asked, "Do you have a second wagon with a side board? I would pick too." Lee said he did. Shane and Winston were going to sleep on the living room floor, giving up their bedroom for Jim. It had been Jim's at one time. After the dishes were done, the house quieted down quickly, Bum being the only protector. An owl in the big cottonwood tree by the front gate hooted Jim to sleep.

The next thing Jim heard was his dad walking down the uncarpeted wooden stairs. It was morning, pre-dawn. An old Leghorn rooster, the chanticleer of the farmyard crowed his greeting. Time to get up. Jim pulled on his coveralls and tiptoed down the stairs to the kitchen where he quenched his thirst with the dipper from the water pail. After stopping at the outhouse Jim caught up with his dad in the barn. Jim started out with Sadie. There was little conversation. Both men were too tired to talk seriously. Production was always less in the morning. They were done milking and separating in a little over an hour. Jim gave the hogs their morning slop. Lee took care of the eggs and poultry feeding, and put two teams of horses in the barn, giving them oats and hay. Breakfast was huge. Ann had gotten up right after the men. She baked raisin muffins, stirred up pancake batter, fried potatoes, salt pork, bacon and left over ham. She scrambled eggs, fried some sliced apples and boiled a huge pot of coffee. You would have thought she was planning to feed a threshing crew. The kids all were at the breakfast table. No one slept in at the Doyers, no one. Lee and Jim were in the barn each currying and harnessing up their team of horses by 8:00.

The men took a large thermos of coffee and a bag of ginger snaps into the field. When they reached the corn, Lee took the first row, Jim right behind him on the next row, horses and wagons to the right, traversing the picked rows, Each man wore a picking knife laced to his left hand. The picker would grab the ear with his right hand then cut the stem of the ear as close to the cob as he could, so the husks would fall off the ear as he tossed it into the wagon. There was little chance of missing with the tall sideboard on the far side of the wagon box. Jim could not keep up with his dad. Lee was way ahead of Jim in no time. The horses very seldom needed to be commanded to move ahead. They knew when the picker was advancing ahead of the wagon, then, would move ahead a few feet, stopping again on their own. When the pickers reached the end of the field they turned 90 degrees left and went cross field. The corn was not in rows in just one direction. It was checked. Lee stopped to rest at 10:00. He was considerably ahead at that time. He walked back to Jim with the coffee and ginger snaps. They both sat on Jim's wagon tongue between his horses to rest their weary legs. Jim stated that he was really enjoying the honest labor of helping his dad. Lee made it clear it was the most satisfying work experience he had in years, being in the field with his son. At the rate they were going, the corn picking would be done by the end of the week. Maybe then they would hunt a few pheasants. They had raised a couple dozen already in the morning. The cornfield had plenty of cover for the birds, patches of grass and other weeds scattered throughout. They had also seen a flock of sharp tailed grouse land in an adjoining oat stubble field. There had always been prairie chickens in the area but they hadn't spotted any yet. They took their teams and wagons at lunchtime. The wagons needed unloading, and the horses needed water. Ann had a big dinner prepared for them; fried chicken, mashed potatoes, green beans, fresh bread. All of this topped off with ground cherry sauce and fresh angel food cake for dessert. It was just the three of them. Priscella was at her in-law's and Shane and Jeanie were at their farm jobs. It was the first day of school for the kids. Winston had elected to go to high school in Voltaire, riding the bus to school each day. He had been an excellent student, graduating number one in his eighth grade. The other children had all walked to their country school down the road. They had each carried their lunch pails filled with ham and rye sandwiches and fresh apples. Jim never thought he could eat what he did after the big breakfast he had in the morning. He had burned up a lot of calories out in the cornfield. Both Lee and Jim lay on the living room floor after dinner for a fifteen-minute nap. After shoveling their loads into the corncrib they went directly back out to the field. A northwest wind came up in the afternoon. An overcast sky added to the discomfort of the day. The men stood out of the wind aside Jim's wagon during their mid-afternoon coffee. Jim wished he had put on long underwear. He would know better tomorrow. Both men had their wagons filled, heaped above the sideboards by 4:30, Lee helped Jim top his off. They were glad to head in. They emptied their wagons before heading into the barn. The cows were waiting in the barnyard. It wouldn't be much longer that Lee would put the cows out to pasture. The grass had nearly stopped growing. In fact Lee had noticed milk production was already falling some. He gave the cows their first silage of the year that evening. They bellowed their appreciation as soon as Lee opened the silo room door. He gave the horses extra oats and hay that evening and did not put them out to pasture. The cows also stayed in that night.

The kids were home from school. When they had completed their homework they came to the barn offering to help, taking their turns at the separator handle, dumping the milk into the separator bowl, pouring a small amount into the cat's dish, not too much or they would give up their mousing. One of the horses had been left harnessed. When the milking was done, Winston hitched it to the sled and slopped the hogs. The younger kids collected the eggs and fed the poultry. Everyone was in the house by 6:30. Ann had fired up the kitchen range with some sticks she had picked up in the grove and a couple shovels of coal. The warmth felt good. It was the first she had filled the coal bucket that fall. Their coal was stored in a separate shed in the back yard a short distance from the house. The coal was obtained from a community mine about three miles away, a surface vein of anthracite. The first settlers had noticed the Native American Indians in the nearby camps sometimes burned coal, particularly after the buffalo disappeared and along with them the buffalo chips. The Indians showed the settlers where the coal was located at the bottom of a depression in a shallow valley. The piece of land was never homesteaded, being kept free for all to harvest for their own needs. One rule, no one could mine to sell. The vein seemed endless. The second rule, no power machinery allowed. Mining was done with a pick and shovel. The supply in Doyer's coal shed, left over from last year, was dwindling. Lee would soon have to replenish it, after he was done picking the corn. Ann had prepared a sumptuous supper; left over chicken, fried potato patties, cream gravy, acorn squash baked in butter and brown sugar and fresh bread, right out of the oven. Ann had brought in the last watermelon out of the garden that afternoon. It was big enough for each to have a piece. There was very little left in the garden, which was just as well, for it wouldn't be long until the first frost. The main topic of conversation after supper was first of all about the goodness of Ann's cooking. Jim couldn't offer enough compliments, and everyone else agreed. Jim was gaining a lot of new fond feelings for Ann, realizing that he had never appreciated her when he was a boy. She was serving as an excellent wife to his dad and mother to the children. Ann denied Jim's comments and blushed a rosy red. Jim well monopolized the evening with his next talk being the joy he was experiencing in being with the family, working with Dad, being treated so well, everyone accepting him just like he was. They asked if there was anything they could do to make his stay more comfortable. He answered, "Just be yourselves! And, by the way, does anyone have any linament? My arm and back muscles are aching terribly from picking corn all day." Ann brought out a bottle of Dr. Askov's Rub, handing it to Winston, telling him, "Go to work." After the rub down, Jim took a hot bath in water heated on the range. He dozed off in the tub till someone knocked on the door asking, "Are you all right? "Yes, fine." He could barely climb the stairs to his bedroom.

Jim fell into the routine of chores, picking corn, eating, talking, sleeping, so different than the hustle and bustle in Janesville. He nearly forgot about his life there. All week, Lee had talked about wanting to go to town. Ann had brought the cream on Tuesday. Now Ann had filled all her empty egg crates. Lee needed some parts for the plow that he wanted to work on before it became too cold to work outside, wanting to get it done before he would need it next spring. Cool weather and a daily breeze to run the windmill, and pump cold water through the cooler was keeping the cream fresh until Saturday morning. Lee and Ann rode in their truck, with the eggs and cream in the truck box. Jim and the five kids rode in his Austin/Healy. Jim took off first, at high speed to thrill the kids. They arranged to meet at the Voltaire Mercantile where Ann had always brought her eggs. She never took cash, always just crediting them to her account. Jim stopped at the Standard Oil Filling Station to fill up his tank, check the oil and put a little air in his tires. The Saturday loafers at the station gave his Austin/Healy the once over. Jim and the kids still arrived at the store before Lee and Ann. The kids headed right for the candy bins, Jim following them. Jim told the proprietor, Mr. Timersson, to give each kid a big paper bag to fill up and he would pay for it all. Jim asked for two bags for himself, one for peanuts, and one for candy. It cost Jim nearly a dollar before they were done. After Lee and Ann arrived and unloaded the eggs, Lee took off for the JOHN DEERE IMPLEMENT STORE. Ann was doing all right with her purchase of staples, so Jim and the kids took off after Lee. Jim wanted to see what was being displayed in the way of the latest tractors. Jim and the kids caught up with Lee sitting on the seat of one of the bright green, yellow trimmed tractors parked out in front of the store, thinking to himself, how much quicker plowing would go next spring if he could do it with a tractor rather than horses, how much easier it would be to grind feed with the tractor belt power, how he wouldn't have to hire a man with a chopper/blower to fill silo, how he could take on that 40 acres across the road from his place that had just come up for rent, if he had a tractor. Jim and the kids stood there watching Lee manipulate the levers and test the foot pedals. He hadn't said a word, but they could read his mind. They all went inside, looked around, chatted for a while, and then left for the hardware store. Jim said to Lee, "How many shot guns do you have? I want to organize a pheasant hunt tomorrow." Lee said "One." Jim stated, "I need four, one for each of us; you, me, Shane and Winston, so I am going to buy three. He bought a Remington Model 11, semiautomatic for himself and two Winchester Model 12, pumps for the boys, all 12 gauges, all modified choke. Next he told the salesclerk to give him a half case of shells, #6 shot, and canvas cases for all the guns. The clerk threw in four free bird carriers. He pulled a roll of bills out of his pants pocket, peeled off a One hundred dollar bill and one Fifty dollar bill, and got very little change back. Lee and the kids stood there with their mouths open. Driving back to the Mercantile, they found Ann standing in front of the store with a huge pile of groceries ready to load in the truck box. They stopped by Shane's work place to invite him to hunt with them the next morning. He accepted heartily. They next stopped at Peterson's, asking them to join in the next day's hunt. They were thrilled agreeing to meet at the Doyers at 9:00 AM.

Jim had done some scouting several evenings during the week to locate a few good pheasant spots. There were plenty; dried up sloughs that had been too wet to plow last spring, all surrounded with picked small grain and corn fields. He had seen plenty of pheasants flying out of corn fields to roost in the tall grass sloughs, and even a few sharp tails and prairie chickens, located mostly in hay fields. Most of the talk that night, while doing chores, was about hunting pheasants. Lee, Winston and Jim arose a little extra early the next morning to be sure and be ready for the hunt. After Shane, Sven and Sven's father arrived, Jim suggested they should all have a short gun safety course and try their skill on a few corncobs. Jim picked up a few cobs by the granary, putting them in a grain bag before they all walked to the other side of the grove. Jim's first order was, no one take their gun off safe nor cock their hammers until they were ready to pull up on a bird. Anyone found walking with their guns off safe or their hammer pulled back would be sent home, on foot. Rule two: Never point your gun in the direction of another hunter. Rule three: Never shoot at birds on the ground. Bum was going to be with them, and it never would be known for sure where he was. Now: line up side to side, I'll throw the corncobs, one shell in a gun at a time. Dad you are first. Load one shell, safe off. Say, "Pull", when you want me to throw the cob. "PULL." Jim threw a cob. Lee was on it, immediately he pulled the trigger, the cob flew into dust. "Good shot!" Next it was Peterson, then Sven, Shane, Winston and last Jim. Shane threw Jim's cob, high. They each shot three rounds. The older men and Jim shot faultlessly. The boys not as well. Bum was barking excitedly the whole time.

Jim suggested they hit the grassy slough by Doyer's pasture first. They took Lee's truck, all riding in the box. They let the Peterson's off on the south end of the slough to

66

post. The other four hunters spread out on the north end to march through about one half of the slough. Bum was dashing with enthusiasm. Pheasant scent was everywhere. A rooster flushed in front of Jim before they had even started to walk. One shot by Jim and the rooster crumpled. Next, the two hens took to the air. Shane tumbled one of them. Jim hollered out, "Let's go easy on the hens to start with." The limit was five birds a piece, three roosters and two hens. The slough was full of birds. Bum was going crazy, but behaving himself by not flushing birds far ahead, out of gun range. When they reached the Petersons, they had twelve birds. Petersons had a number of birds fly by them. They had shot two a piece. The hunters next worked the other half of the slough, not bothering to post anyone on the end. That drive yielded seven more birds. They decided to go to the Petersons farm next. They had a big slough along side a creek that ran through their place. On the way they saw a flock of sharp tails land in a stubble wheat field. Lee drove into the field a ways. All the hunters piled out of the truck, walked a few yards and found themselves right in the midst of a big flock of sharp tails. Everyone shot till his or her guns were empty. They had fourteen birds to pick up. Everyone was thrilled. By the time they finished working the Petersons slough, they had seven more pheasants, reaching their limit, and were running low on shells. It was dinnertime. They drove back to Doyers. Ann had prepared a light lunch, anticipating a pheasant dinner for the evening meal. After lunch everyone participated in cleaning the birds. It only took about an hour. Lee and Peterson said they had enough shooting for the day. Jim and the other boys said they wanted more. Jim took them to a spot he knew would be good. The others started calling Shane a *hen shooter* and said they could shoot their own hens. It was all in good spirits but Shane never lost that label.

The boys drove to Petersons, cleaned the rest of the birds and left them there. Lee had started chores when they returned to the Doyer place. They all pitched in and were done before dinnertime. Jim stopped by his auto on the way to the house, opened up the trunk and dug out a bottle of his brandy. When he washed up and entered the kitchen he sat it in the middle of the table, then poured him a shot into a tumbler. Ice was unheard of. He put a little water in the glass with a dipper, tipped his chair back, sipped his drink and said, "This is living!" Lee soon came in, surprised to see the brandy bottle, he said, "Where did you get that?" Jim said, "From a friend in Wisconsin. Have a drink, dad." They each had several. They loosened up, talked a storm, even talking Ann into one drink. She loosened up too. The pheasant was savory, the brandy better yet. The bottle was put away after dinner. Just as well. Lee was not to good about knowing when to quit.

Jim got into the routine of working with his dad the next week. The cornfield was thirty acres. At the rate they were going, with two of them picking every day and with the weather staying halfway decent they were going to be done picking the field by the end of the week. As they closed in on the last few rows Friday morning they were jubilant over their accomplishment. Another reason for joy; they had flushed more pheasants out of the remnant standing corn than they thought existed in all of McHenry County. At noon meal that day Jim announced that he would like to go to town the next day and to also hunt pheasants again on Sunday. "Does anyone object?" They answered in unison, "No way do we object." Then Ann spoke up, "I do not object, but there is one more thing I would like to add to the schedule. There is a barn dance at the Kelly McGraw's on Sunday night that I would like all of us to go to. Does anyone object? No one objected. In fact there were many affirmative comments. Saturday morning, Jim told Lee to meet him and the kids at the John Deere Implement Dealership after Lee had dropped Ann off at the grocery store. First Jim and the kids stopped at the grocery store and loaded up with candy, then went directly to the Implement store. The same tractor that had been out front the previous

1927 JOHN DEERE MODEL "D" TRACTOR

week was still there. Jim went inside and asked the dealer about it. The dealer said it was a 1927 Model D. The price was $835. How much extra for the three bottom plow that was attached to it? $145. Hoe much for the silage chopper/blower operated by the power pulley on the tractor? $125 Jim said," That's $1,115 all together, give me a deal and I will buy all three." The dealer got a piece of paper and a pencil, did some figuring for a minute and answered, "1,050." "I'll take it," said Jim, and he took a roll out of his pocket, opened it up, took a thousand dollar bill from the inside of the roll and a fifty from the outside and handed them to the dealer. The kids watched the whole deal with mouths open and eyes popping. Winston said, "What are you going to do with a tractor Jim? His response, "It isn't mine, Its your dad's" Lee had just walked in. He heard his name and asked what was going on. Kim piped up excitedly, "JJJJJJJJim jjjjust bbbbought yyyyyou aaa ttttrractor." Kim ordinarily didn't stutter but with what had just happened he couldn't stop his teeth form chattering. Jim said, "That's right, Dad. The one out front, you drive it home. Be sure there is fuel in it. The dealer said he would throw in a full tank of fuel and a tank mounted on legs to store fuel in on the farm, free. He also said he would deliver the plow, silage chopper/blower and tank to the farm, hauling them out on his flat bed this same afternoon. That was the first Lee had heard of the plow and silage machine. He said, "Jim, Jim, Jim, you should not have done all this." Jim said, "Shut up and drive your tractor home, we will let Ann know. In fact, Ann and the rest of us may be a little late in getting home. Don't worry about us." The dealer went with Lee to fill the fuel tank on the tractor and give Jim a few instructions on the Model D. Winston hopped into Lee's truck, the rest got in Jim's Austin/Healy. They all drove back to the Mercantile. The kids ran in to tell Ann about Lee's new Model D tractor that Jim had bought him. They loaded all of Ann's groceries into the back seat of the Austin/Healy as Jim ordered Ann into the front seat. Jim told Winston to follow him and for Mary to get into the truck with her brother to keep him company, they were all going to drive to Velva. It was a larger town than Voltaire, over a thousand people, just four miles northwest on highway #52. Jim had found out that the hardware store there carried kerosene-operated refrigerators. As they pulled up in front of Velva hardware, no one but Jim knew the reason they were visiting the store. He told them all to come in the store with them. He walked directly to a display of General Electric Refrigerators, mostly electrified models with the big round refrigeration units on the top, but on the end of the display was a refrigerator with a different configuration, sitting further away from the wall because of a kerosene burner and tank on the back side. Jim stopped in front of this unusual appliance, Ann and the kids behind. Jim opened the door, put his hand inside. The interior was cool. Jim invited Ann and the kids to feel the coolness. Everyone was amazed. *Cold from heat*! A modern day miracle. It even had an ice cube-making compartment. Jim had seen this kind of refrigerator before, located behind the bars in several of his rural customer's establishments without electricity, reducing their dependency on ice to cool their beverages. This type of appliance was quite new on the market. There was a price tag on the front of the unit, $74.39. A clerk came over to the group as they were all admiring the appliance, asking them if he could wait on them. Jim said, "Yes, do you have one of these kerosene operated refrigerators still unpacked, in the shipping crate?" The clerk said, "Yes, we certainly do." Jim asked, "Will you help us load it on our truck and furnish some rope to secure it for the trip home?" Jim took a bundle of money out of his pocket, peeled off a hundred dollar bill and gave it to the clerk. All these recent purchases hadn't seemed to reduce the size of Jim's roll. The clerk said "We will load it immediately." Jim told Winston to back the truck up to the loading platform on the back side of the store, then asked the clerk if he would throw in some small gauge stove pipe, at no extra charge, that would be needed to vent the burner. He said he would. All this time, Ann, stood awe struck, finally saying, "Jim you are too generous. I did not know you were so wealthy." Jim said, "I am not wealthy. I make a lot of money, but I am not wealthy, and you know why I am not wealthy? Because I spend my money instead of saving it." Ann then put her arms around Jim as she said, "Thank you, thank you for everything." After loading the refrigerator, it was getting past lunchtime, so, Jim took them all to the Velva Blue Café for noon lunch, hot beef sandwiches with mashed potatoes and gravy. For beverage, they all had fountain coke, a change from traditional milk at home. All were in high spirits. What a day.

Lee was home when they arrived at the farm, with the top speed of 4-5 miles per hour not taking him long, even though he had to run on the shoulders to avoid digging up the road with the lugs. He was running all around the yard with his tractor like a child with a new toy, a grin on his face a mile wide. At first, they all thought he had gotten to the brandy bottle.

Shane was home so they had plenty of help getting the new refrigerator into the kitchen and before long into its place, vent properly installed, burner lit and starting to cool.

Everyone was constantly opening the door and placing their hand inside, testing the progress of the cooling process. It was slow but steady.

Jim didn't help with the chores that night. There were plenty of other hands. He had been putting off a visit to his mother's grave. It had been foremost on his mind ever since he had first planned the trip back to North Dakota. He telephoned the Peterson's asking Priscella if she would go with him, She was pleased to accompany him on his mission. Their mother, Elizabeth, was buried in the graveyard at the South Voltaire Episcopal Church, the Doyer family's place of worship. The Peterson's farm was on the way to the church. Jim stopped there to pick up Priscella. The entire household came out to the car when he stopped. They knew of his purchases that day. Ann had telephoned them while he was on the way over. They all expressed compliments to him for being so generous. Jim downplayed the gifts.

Priscella was pleased that Jim had asked her to visit the cemetery with him. It was near sunset when they parked their car by the church and walked into the cemetery, a beautiful evening, with a net of clouds in the western sky beginning to cover the sun, turning deep blue and orange-pink, a setting for nostalgia, a time for Jim to repine. Priscella knew the location of the grave. She led them to it. The headstone was a simple flat piece of granite, some sunken in the ground, the edges covered with weed and grass. Jim had to clear the edges with his hands to read the inscription:

ELIZABETH PRISCELLA DOYER
June 3rd 1889-September 16th 1921

Jim said, "Priscella, did you know it was six years ago today that mother passed away? I did. Mother and I were very, very close. We never had a bitter word with each other. She was always encouraging me to dream, dream plans for my future, plans I shared with no one else. When she died I was left entirely alone. Even you, as much as I respected you, could not serve as my confidant. That is why I ran away from home. I was living in a cocoon. I needed to burst out, to escape, and that is what I did, and with reasonable success. But, you know, Priscella, I don't think I have yet satisfied my urge to emerge. You know I have developed a very successful automobile service business in Janesville, but that wasn't enough. I had connections to the underground, servicing the automobiles of the Mafia bootleggers. Soon the Sicilian Mafiosa Don offered me a position in his organization. I accepted it. This seemed to satisfy my urge to burst out. It became my debauchery. I have reveled in it, but not allowed it to intoxicate me. I thank my dear mother for all of this." He then fell silent. Priscella could barely see in the twilight that there were tears in his eyes. She dabbed them with her handkerchief. They stood by their mother's headstone for quite a while, as daylight dwindled, neither uttering another word till they were back in the car, driving down the road. Jim then asked Priscella if she would ride to Velva with him next week to arrange for an upright monument to replace the flat marker on their mother's grave. He had seen a monument works there. She promised she would go with him.

The pheasant hunt the next day matched one of a week previous. The hunters even got into a flock of prairie chickens. Ann put the cleaned birds in her new refrigerator to save them for some day the next week. She thought everyone would get plenty to eat at the barn dance in the evening. A potluck supper was being served along with the dance. Ann had been assigned to bring a potato/ham hot dish. Everyone went to the dance, children of all ages, singles, couples, and old folks. Age was no barrier. There were two bands; an old time group, really old time, who played nothing but waltzes and square dances. The other band played music of the Terrible Twenties, including scores for the most popular dance of the day, the Charleston. The two bands alternated on the band stage. The table for food was made of saw horses and planks. There must have been a hundred dishes. Coffee, milk, and lemonade were on a separate table. Jim noticed some of the men spent quite a lot of time out in the yard. He investigated and found them to be nipping on bottles of home brew. He dug in the trunk of his car and brought out the last remaining three bottles of his brandy. He passed it around, loosing up the dancers considerably. Before long it was gone. Jim danced mostly with Ann and his sisters, only several fox trots with a sampling of many of the single girls attending. He could have any number of dances, being considered the most eligible bachelor there. The bands quit playing at 2:00 AM. Many of the small children, by that time were asleep in the bales of hay. The last of the crowd did not depart until 3:00 AM, finishing up the last of the food before departing.

Jim spent the first two days of the next week overhauling dad's truck. It purred like a kitten when he was done with it. Wednesday, Jim and Priscella went to the monument works in Velva. They picked out a beautiful stone made out of Minnesota Pink granite, instructing the carver to place the family name. DOYER on the top, on both sides, with Mother's name and dates on the left side of the surface towards the grave, with Dad's name on the right with his birth date only. Lee had bought two adjacent plots when Elizabeth died. The carver said he would not be able to set the stone until spring. Jim paid him. Next Jim stopped on main-street in front of the Velva Millinery. He asked Priscella to come inside. At first she refused, saying, "I look to raggedly to go into such a fancy place." Jim insisted. When they were inside, Jim asked the clerk to bring out the fanciest, finest winter coat they had in stock, one that would look nice on his sister. The clerk came back with a heavy wool garment, regal purple in color, trimmed with a high collar and cuff's made of silver fox, lined with imported black silk. Jim told the clerk to have Priscella try it on. Jim then stood back a ways, admiring his sister as she turned around in front of a huge mirror. "Sister, you are a beauty," he said. To the clerk he said, "If you have a hat trimmed with the same fur, we will buy both the hat and coat. The clerk brought out a matching hat, and then wrapped them both in a lovely box. Priscella said, "Where will I ever wear such a fine ensemble this winter?" Jim said, "Everywhere, church services, funerals, weddings, school programs, dances, shopping, everywhere. Promise me!" She promised.

Jim had met one of his old school buddies, Vince O'Leary, at the dance, a member of the gang that loitered with Jim on the way home from school years ago. They had talked of hunting. Vince had preferred duck hunting. He invited Jim to go with him next Saturday morning. He picked Jim and Bum up at 2:00 AM, boat loaded on a trailer behind his pickup. They headed south to the lake country in McLean County, just north of the town of Turtle Lake. Nearby were Strawberry Lake, Long Lake, Crooked Lake, Lake Williams, Blue Lake, Brush Lake and Peterson Lake. Vince preferred a spot between Blue Lake and Peterson Lake, where he anticipated they should get some pass shooting. The wind was strong from the northwest. It should keep the ducks moving between the two lakes and from the lakes to the stubble wheat fields where the ducks were feeding. It was pitch dark yet when they arrived at the lakes. Vince had previously constructed a blind out of brush and cattails on the north shore of Lake Peterson. They patched it up a bit, hid the boat and pickup under a tree, threw two dozen mallard decoys in the lake a few yards off shore, crawled into the blind and pulled out their thermos jugs, some cookies and a few stories of the good old days. It was just becoming light in the east. Heavy clouds filled the sky overhead and hung on the horizon all around them. The wind was to their backs, where it should be. The ducks should come in to them off the lake, wings beating hard against the wind, easy targets whether their attraction was the decoys or if there intention was to fly right over them to Blue Lake behind their blind. Either way, they would be flying slower against the wind. While it was still too dark to shoot the men could see silhouettes of birds rising off the lake. As some birds came in closer to the shore, where the men were blinded, they could hear the "quack! Quack! Quack!" of hen mallards. Several minutes later, a flock of two dozen snuck in and sat down in the decoys, landing before either Jim or Vince noticed. Vince spotted them first; he nudged Jim, both men stood up. The mallards jumped straight up off the water like they had been launched by springs. The two men shot, two plump drakes fell. Before second shots could be fired, the birds had climbed high into the wind, carrying them away like loose kites. Jim called "Fetch!" to Bum. He jumped out of the blind and swam right towards one of the downed ducks. It wasn't easy going on the way back to shore, against the wind and whipped waves. When he reached shore he dropped the duck and shook himself, then picked the bird back up, ran into the blind and dropped it at Jim's feet. Jim said, "Good boy, but you aren't done yet. There is another one out there." Jim pointed his hand in the direction of the lake, but Bum did not understand. Jim then picked up a rock and threw it the direction of the other downed duck, which by now had been carried out to the lake for a considerable distance. It had become difficult to see in the dim light with the waves so high. Bum, however, kept going until he finally spotted it, caught up with it and brought it back in. He lay right down after dropping the bird, resting quite a while before moving a muscle. As it became light, the men could see that both Blue Lake and Lake Peterson were full of ducks. They had birds flying into them all morning, some into the decoys, some low over the blind to Blue Lake. Both Jim and Vince concentrated on the birds passing over them so the downed birds would fall on land, easier retrieves for Bum. Most of the birds were mallards but they did bag a few green winged teals and pintails. The men ate lunch about 10:00 that morning. Vince had brought ham sandwiches, Jim pieces of roast pheasant, apple pie and chocolate cake for dessert. They had their limit of birds before noon. When they reached home they were up late cleaning them, using the time honored stripping method, dipping them in wax after removing the feathers. The soft down and feathers were all saved, stuffed in a gunny sack, hung on the clothes line to be aired for weeks, stuffing for pillows to be made some cold winter day that following winter.

Everyone was both tired of hunting and eating pheasant, so the entire family went to church Sunday morning, except Jim. It didn't fit his makeup. Ann had placed the ducks in the huge roaster, early that morning, all ten, Jim's half of the hunt, stuffing the cavities with pieces of apple and some dried prunes. Strips of bacon had been laid across the breasts of the birds. While Ann was in church, it was Jim's job to feed the fire in the range with just the right amount of wood to keep the oven temperature about 400 degrees. He sat right in the kitchen where he could keep an eye on things, dozing off once and nearly falling off his chair. When the family got home, Ann complimented Jim on a job well done. The ducks were baked to perfection. Ann had brought a large cabbage up out of the cellar that was to serve as the main side dish. A large bowl of warm, brown sugar raisin muffins with home churned butter dripping off them sat in the center of the table. Everyone ate voraciously all exclaiming their delight in the roast wild duck, better then their barnyard ducks, a stronger, wilder taste. The whole roaster full disappeared. Then the surprise of the meal, homemade peach/vanilla ice cream produced in the new GE refrigerator. The peach flavor came from a jar of Ann's preserves she had made during the summer. The Voltaire Mercantile carried Washington State peaches shipped in by rail every year during season. The cream called for in the recipe from the Doyer heard, rich and fresh from that morning's milking. Jim took one heck of a long nap after dinner. He was worn out from the previous day's duck hunt.

Lee announced at breakfast Monday morning that he was going to build a machine shed. He couldn't stand to have his new tractor outside all winter. All there was now was a garage for the truck. The new building was going to be 20' x 60' with double sliding doors on both ends, no windows, bigger than needed for the tractor and silage/chopper blower. But, he knew there would be other machines bought in the future, such as a corn picker and a feed grinder operated by the tractor power pulley. There was no end of new machines coming on the market. He planned to build a machine shop, with insulated walls, as a lean to on the south side of the machine shed. That would have windows and a barrel stove in it for heat in cold weather. Jim said, "I would like to help you get started, Dad. I am planning to have to leave on Thursday." Everyone gulped when Jim talked about leaving. They did not want to believe his stay would end. After a pause Lee answered, "OK, we'll go to town with the truck. What materials we can not haul, we'll have the lumber yard bring it out here today." By afternoon, they were staking out the foundation, they had no transit, doing it with a chalk line, a carpenter's square and a plumb. Holes for the footings and trenches for the foundation were dug by hand. Winston pitched in to help when he got home from school. Kim, being 12, was of some help too. Jim kept at the job till dark before knocking off to help Lee finish chores. At the supper table that night, Lee talked expansively about his plans. He had found out on Sunday that he was going to be able to rent the forty acres of land across the road. So he had his own 160, Ann's 160 and now the 40. 360 acres was a large farm, but he knew he could do it, particularly now with a tractor. Winston had committed himself to continue helping his dad after school and on vacations. Kim was also becoming a willing hand. Ann was supportive and helpful at every turn. He had been willing to sell over half of his wheat crop that fall at a good price, keeping what he needed for the poultry and livestock. Ann had marketed her spring roosters, except what she kept for the family's own need. She was getting a good price for her eggs. Cream was bringing an exceptionally good price at the creamery and Lee's cows were high on the butterfat test. The cream check every month was good. Lee had 25 hogs nearly ready. The market on pork was high. Lee mentioned another plan of his. Next spring, instead of marketing his bull calves, he was going to have them castrated and feed them up for market. He would have the necessary feed with additional acreage. The Doyer's had a little money in the bank. The future looked good. Lee turned to Jim, over their second cups of coffee and asked, "Jim, do you ever think about coming back to North Dakota to get into farming? If you do, would you consider joining me, or at least farming nearby so we could share machinery and labor? The question took Jim by surprise. "Dad, number one: you probably couldn't put up with me on a long term basis. Number two: I had never thought of the possibility. Number three: I take your invitation as a very high compliment. No, I think I had better go back to Wisconsin and do what I have been doing. It has worked out well for me. But, who knows what the future holds. We will cross those bridges when we get to them. It's been great to be here for a month, given me a new lease on life. I am truly rejuvenated, thanks to you all, and particularly you, Ann, for your cooking, and the help you receive from Jeanie, Mary, Amy and Helen." Ann said, "God bless you son." Lee said, "We are proud of you son." Winston said "Amen." The other kids laughed. Good feelings saturated the room.

Next day Lee and Jim laid the footings and foundation for the machine shed, using cement block. They covered their work with straw that evening, in fear of frost on the concrete, not yet set. The weather was remaining remarkably good. They started to raise the walls on Wednesday; slow with no power equipment, sawing all the 2x4s and 2x6s with a hand saw. Jim was worried about his dad being alone on the job when he left the next day. He made his dad promise to have a neighbor come over and help, particularly with the roof. Ann made supper into a going away party that night with ice cream, and a frosted angel food cake, confectioners candy sprinkled into letters that said **GOOD LUCK JIM!** . Sven and Priscella were there to join in. Jim took Priscella aside and pressed a hundred dollar bill into her hand, telling her to use it to buy Christmas presents for the children. She thanked him with a big kiss on the lips. Jim slept restlessly that night. It was not going to be easy leaving his family the next morning. He wondered if the transition into his other life was going to be troublesome. Priscella was the only one whom he spoke to about his job in the underworld. He had no reason to talk of it to anyone else. He knew Priscella would keep it to herself. He helped Lee with the chores in the morning, walked down the lane with Winston to meet his school bus, gave the kids a ride to their school in his Austin/Healey, then ate a big breakfast with Lee and Ann before hitting the road. There were no tears. Jim promised to not wait five years for his next visit. There had been a sprinkle of rain during the night so his departure down the road was dust free. Lee and Ann, arm in arm, watched Jim's Austin/Healey till it was out of sight. Ann said, "Jim is sure a fine young man, but he has a mysterious nature, hard for me to figure out." Lee responded, "I agree. There are some things about him that I do not understand. Priscella seems to be the only one that really knows him. They are very close to each other." Jim did not drive through Voltaire that morning, instead turned east at the first corner, the route he had taken to Bergen the morning he ran away five years ago. He noted the cotton wood grave along the South Branch of the Mouse River where he had secreted himself, while waiting for the freight train into Bergen, that he jumped to hitch his ride to Valley City. Even to this day he considered it a clever escape. Jim took his time on the road that morning, stopping by for lunch at a café in Carrington. While driving, he reminisced about his boyhood on the farm, how different it had been now for the month he was home. It amazed him how he and his father had related to each other now, as compared to years ago, just because they both made an effort to support each other rather that antagonize each other. Good human relations can be so simple and enjoyable when the mortals involved make an effort to love, admire and help each other. Jim had learned a great lesson this last month.

CHAPTER SEVEN

That afternoon Clutch checked into the Valley City Hotel. From there he drove over to the old shop for another, longer visit with Sparky. Clutch concluded, unequivocally, that everything was going well with Sparky. No question, his family life was happy. He and his wife had two children, which she brought down to the shop for a visit, to show them off. The shop itself was prospering. That was evident to Clutch. A glance around reveled considerable new equipment and Sparky's staff was busy. Clutch telephoned Joe from Sparky's shop, asking he and Trudy out to dinner. He accepted, calling Trudy telling her that Clutch was in town and to put on her finest for a night out. Jim had heard about a new supper club several miles south of Valley City in the little town of Fingal. In fact his old friend, Fig Corcione, had mentioned the place the last time he and Clutch visited. The club was one of Fig's new customers and was very popular in the Valley City area, thanks to an appreciative Barnes County Sheriff. Clutch picked up Joe and Trudy at their home. Clutch mentioned the Fingal Supper Club. Joe had never been there but had heard of it. Trudy expressed apprehensively, "Are you sure it's all right, Clutch. Clutch said, laughingly, "If Joe can't protect you, I will." The parking lot of the club was filled when they arrived. Jim asked the man that met them at the door if he was the proprietor. He said he was. Clutch introduced himself as a friend of Fiagio (Fig) Corcione. The proprietor was slow to respond, not knowing whom he was talking to, suspicious of Clutch being an undercover agent. Clutch mentioning that he at one time had been a co-owner of Clutch and Sparky's Automotive Repair Shop put the proprietor at ease. He had been a long time customer of the shop and remembered when Clutch started the business. He even remembered playing pool with Clutch at the Main

Street Pool Hall in Valley City. The conversation lightened considerably. The proprietor said, "Remember my name, BoBo Alfonso." Clutch said, "Yes, now I do." Clutch introduced BoBo to Joe and Trudy then asked if they could get a seat in the back lounge. "Of, Course!" BoBo motioned another man to take his position at the front door, then brought the three to the lounge himself, opening the door with a key, seating them at a back table, sitting down with them himself, ordering a round of drinks from the fetching, buxom, blond waitress, which he told her were on the house. Jim said, "How are you getting along with the sheriff?" BoBo answered, "Fine, that's him seated there at the next table." Whispering, "His whole night is on the house." BoBo left to assume his position at the front door. Trudy commented that the back room was larger and more crowded that the front room. Jim said, "Same menu except for the spirits." Steaks were the predominant items. After the three had a second drink, "Blondie" took their order. Clutch and Joe had New York strips, Trudy a filet, all ordered rare. They were the best. Clutch thought of stopping at the sheriff's table on the way out, but didn't want to embarrass him. The hour was late when they arrived at Joe and Trudy's house. They invited Clutch in, but he declined. They all said loving "goodbyes", hoping they could be together again soon.

Clutch did not get an early start the next morning. The long drive and night out had tired him. He had no business to do in Minneapolis so he stopped sixty miles west in the town of Litchfield, checking into the Lenhardt Hotel. Clutch inquired if there was a drink available in town. Mr. Lenhardt himself was at the desk. His answer was emphatic. "No! You can get an excellent dinner in our dining room, but no liquor." Clutch noted a pool hall across the street. He walked over to it, inquired about a drink, but received the same answer. He decided the town was "dry", too many Scandinavians who did not know how to have fun.

It was late when Clutch arrived at his apartment in Janesville the next night. He was up early the next day, Saturday, and at the shop right after breakfast. Everything had gone well while he was gone. Oh, there had been a couple of bad eggs who had not wanted to pay their entire bill, claiming it was too high for the work done. Clutch's foreman would not let them have their cars until payment was made. The response was rough language and threats but the foreman held his ground. One finally paid up, but the other car was still parked at the back end of the shop. Clutch said, "I'll talk to him if he comes back." Sure enough the car owner showed up that morning. Clutch tried to reason with the man. The man became verbally abusive. He called Clutch a "son of a bitch", which really riled Clutch, telling the man to pay up or leave the premises. The man continued ranting. Clutch called for his foreman to come to the office with two other mechanics, one an amateur wrestler, who put an arm lock on the man and ushered him out the front door. Clutch was wary of the man returning at night to do damage to the shop. He thought it best to protect the interests of the shop by telephoning the city police and asking them to intensify their surveillance of the shop that night. Clutch's suspicions were justified. The police telephoned Clutch's apartment at 3:00 AM to inform him that they had apprehended the man, catching him in the act of attempting to break into the shop through the back door. The police were going to charge him with forceful entry with intent to rob or do damage. Clutch eventually learned the man was convicted in court and received a stiff jail sentence. The man had not picked up his car after three months. Clutch had it sold at a public auction. Clutch rewarded the police by purchasing a very generous number of tickets for all his employees to the upcoming Policemen's Ball.

The next day being Sunday, Clutch decided to drive down to Lake Geneva and visit Don Sigarto Bellagio. The guards at the estate's gate stopped Clutch but when they saw who he was, they allowed him right in. There were certain people who did not need clearance by the Don, Clutch being one of them. As Clutch drove around to the front of the mansion, the Don came right out on the patio to greet him, throwing his arms around Clutch in grand welcome, saying, "It's so good to have you back, Clutch Doyer, you are bronzed and deeply etched from the outdoor life." Clutch said, "Why, has there been trouble?" "No, no, I've just missed you. You are my favorite Captain. How was North Dakota? How was your family?" Clutch answered, "Everything and everyone were fine. It was a good change for me, a repast of restoration. It was good for both myself, and my family. Now I am ready to get back to work. I have already straightened out several things at my shop. Have you any tough problems for me?" The Don said, "Yes, maybe there is. You are aware of the problem we had several years ago in regards to liquor coming into the United States on the ships docking in Duluth and Superior and are having finally gained the control we needed over that supply. You may also recall at that time we pretty much ignored the small amount of liquor being smuggled across the Ontario and Manitoba borders into Minnesota and North Dakota. Unfortunately, it has been increasing to the point where we are going to have to do something about it. Fiagio (Fig) Corcione, my North Dakota agent, tells me he has been running into some competition. Clutch told Sig about his visit to the Fingal Supper Club, where he had been so well received by the proprietor. Clutch said he had doubts about the Fingal Club receiving supplies from anybody but Fig. Sig said, "That may be, but don't be too sure." Clutch thought for a while, and then offered a plan, "I know a lot of people in Valley City. I will telephone somebody and have them stake out the Fingal Club and the proprietors house for a few nights to see if the club is receiving shipments from other than Fig's men. We'll find out." Sig sanctioned the plan, then went on to tell Clutch he was really more concerned about buyers further north, in cities nearer the Manitoba border; Grand Forks, Devils Lake, Rugby, Minot, and even Williston. The syndicate had put a man on that route nearly six months ago and he had not been doing as well as he should. Sig said he had information that non-syndicate smuggling routes were being changed every day, using border crossings on back country dirt roads that traversed border farms, where a little payoff to the farmer would keep him from asking any questions, and his maybe even being of help with his horses at times to pull booze laden automobiles through mud holes and snow drifts. These tactics made it very difficult for either the border patrol or competitive bootleggers to put a finger on the "border crossing runners". Sig said, "Clutch I may need your help. Let's wait to see what you come up with at the Fingal Club. For now, we need to get our minds off business. I challenge you to a game of billiards. My wife and the children are in Racine shopping for the day. I know the cook is planning lunch, I'll tell her we have a guest. Sig talked Clutch into staying the entire weekend. He told Clutch that a business associate and a girl friend from Chicago were coming in the afternoon to also spend the weekend, but there were plenty of bedrooms for all. Interestingly, the man from Chicago brought two beautiful young ladies. Clutch suspected Sig had telephoned his business associate, telling him to bring an extra gal. Sig was perpetually concerned that Clutch was single. The three couples went out for a big time event that evening, to a fancy dinner club with a liquor lounge and dance floor. A blues group played on the bandstand. Clutch hadn't such a wild time for ages.

Sunday was a lazy day at the Bellagio Estate. Everyone slept late. Clutch had slept with his Chicago girl friend. She wasn't bad, although she looked better the night before than the next morning. Clutch went for a long walk after he had eaten his breakfast. He had been pondering the complexities of his life non-stop lately. He was at it again as he strolled through the woods again this morning. He had a great time on the farm visiting his family but now he was very challenged again by attacking the problem Sig was confronting him with. He would leave for northern North Dakota in a minute, if Sig requested it. Lunch was tomato soup and a variety of imported and domestic cheeses with fresh hard crust bread and rich creamery butter. Fresh fruit was offered for dessert. Clutch left early for Janesville. That night he telephoned Joe at his home in Valley City to discuss the Fingal Supper Club. Joe said since they had dinner there he had found out more about BoBo. His home was in Valley City, not too far from Joe's home. There were other people with money invested in the club beside BoBo. Joe accepted the request by Clutch to get information about he source of the club's liquor. Joe was somewhat puzzled as to Clutch's interest. He promised him he would explain it sometime, probably quite soon. Joe said he would get some of the men at work to assist him. Clutch said they would all be paid for their services.

One week later, Joe telephoned Clutch. He had the information Clutch wanted. BoBo received his shipments of liquor that night at the club, about 4:00 AM, nearly every other night, that frequency not being unusual, what with the ever present fear of such establishments being raided and their not wanting to lose a large stock of liquor. The deliveries were all made with a truck driven by a man Joe recognized as an employee of Fig Corcione, with one exception, last Friday night when the delivery was made by a truck with a strange driver. Painted on both doors of the truck was the name MINOT POP COMPANY.

Clutch visited Don Sigarto Bellagio the next day. The Don was now convinced his suspicions were justified. He requested that Clutch, with two of the Don's men leave for North Dakota with out delay to find out where the Canadian liquor was coming across the border. The two men picked Clutch up early the next morning at his apartment, driving Sig's personal car, his supercharged Alfo Romeo imported from Italy. Clutch recognized the car, it having been in his shop several times. They headed right out, going through Minneapolis before noon, ending up in Fargo, North

Dakota for the night. They visited a super club that evening in the small town of Riverside, just west of Fargo. They introduced themselves to the proprietor, identifying themselves as being with the Bellagio Syndicate and their being aware of his establishment being one of the Syndicate's customers. The proprietor invited Clutch and Sig's two henchmen to the locked liquor lounge in the back of the club. The proprietor ordered a round of drinks, while all visited on causal topics. With the start of the second round of drinks, everyone more relaxed and loose, Clutch explained his mission, and then asked outright, "Sir, do you buy liquor from any other supplier than our Syndicate?" Unhesitatingly, the proprietor said, "No, none whatsoever!!" Clutch then said, "Do you know of anyone in the area selling Canadian liquor or has anyone approached you offering to sell you Canadian liquor?" The proprietor did not come right out with an answer. While the proprietor paused, Clutch and the two henchmen stared at him motionlessly. He knew from the silence that he better have an answer. His story was this: One night when he returned home, after closing the supper club, he noticed a truck parked around the corner from his house. By the time he had pulled into his driveway, the truck had come around the corner and parked right behind him in the driveway. A man jumped out, saying he wanted to talk to the supper club proprietor. The man at first indulged in commonplace conversation; "How's business at the supper club? How's your family? Hasn't it been nice weather?" Then he put the real question to the proprietor, "Who do you buy your liquor from?" The proprietor said, "I gave him a vague answer, not identifying the Bellagio Syndicate. He pushed me for an answer. I did not like that." Finally he got to the point. He wanted to sell me some Canadian Whisky. I told him I had a deal with my present supplier that I did not want to violate. He pushed me some more, even suggesting I may be heading for trouble if I didn't do business with him. That infuriated me. I told him to leave my premises. He hopped in his truck and drove away. Clutch asked the club proprietor if he noticed any name on the side of the truck. He said, Yes, MINOT POP COMPANY was painted on both doors." Clutch said, "That's all I wanted to know. Thank you. Go on about your business. We are going to order dinner."

 Clutch and the two men drove to Minot the next morning. They had no trouble finding the MINOT POP COMPANY, located on the east edge of town. Parked out in back was a truck with the company name on both doors. Right across the street were Green Gable Tourist Cabins. Clutch and the two henchmen rented one, parking the Alfo Romeo out of sight behind the cabin. The location offered them an excellent opportunity keep the pop factory under surveillance. The truck left several times during the day to make deliveries of pop to local establishments, there being nothing suspicious about that. Clutch and the two henchmen followed the truck in their Alfo Romeo, remaining a discreet distance behind to avoid being seen. The two henchmen were good at that type of hustle. There was a hamburger shop down the street a block from the Green Gable Cabins. One of the henchmen walked to it late afternoon for some hamburgers and pop for Clutch and the two men. A little later, the truck driver from the pop factory came out and likewise walked down to the hamburger shop. He stayed there a while, obviously eating in. By now it was dusk, soon to become dark. When he returned to the pop factory, he climbed right into his truck and drove towards the city center. Clutch and the two henchmen bolted out of the cabin, into the Alfo Romeo and followed, safely disconnected from the truck. At city center, the pop truck turned north onto the road leading to the border town of Antler. The truck driver would have difficulty noticing his followers. The Alfo Romeo was specially fitted with lights, shaded to direct the beams only onto the road directly in front. Over and hour later, having driven straight north for fifty miles, the pop truck drove into the small town of Antler, just two miles south of the Canadian border. At that juncture the pop truck turned west on a very narrow slightly graveled road, went about three miles, then turned north on a dirt road. After less than a mile, it pulled off the road stopping in a cottonwood grove along a creek bed. There was a full moon shining in the southeast sky, fully illuminating the landscape. Clutch and his two men were a good half mile behind the pop truck and at this point had turned their lights completely off. They moved the Alfo Romeo forward slowly another one-fourth mile, and then drove off the road themselves, stopping behind a haystack just off the dirt road. Clutch had earlier inquired and found out there were official border control crossings about every ten to twenty five miles on the North Dakota/Canadian border. There was one north of Antler that closed at 10:00 PM but none at the border crossing on the dirt road they had now been traveling. They were in no mans land. The border between official crossings was patrolled by horse-mounted officers, but very uncommonly. After about a half hour wait, Clutch noted a dim pair of headlights approaching from the north. The vehicle pulled off the road into the cottonwood grove where the pop truck was parked. The two drivers quickly transferred a large number of boxes from the Canadian truck to the pop truck. At this time, Clutch and his two men got out of their auto, the men each with a Thompson sub-machine gun in hand, Clutch with his .38 caliber side arm in hand, all three with black hoods over their heads, with narrow slits for their eyes. The pop truck pulled back onto the dirt road, headed south to where Clutch and his two men were hunkered down in the grass alongside the road. When the pop truck was but a few feet away, the two henchmen opened fire with their Tommy guns, directing their fire towards the left hand side mounted gas tank. The tank exploded with a FLASH! Nearly engulfing Clutch and his men. Had they been five feet closer they themselves would have been sacrificed in the inferno. The hoods protected their faces from being flash burned. The truck veered off the road to the right, coming to a halt some distance from the road. Within minutes it was consumed, all but the frame and the engine block. Clutch and his men wasted no time, getting into the Alfo Romeo and speeding back down the route into Antler and heading for Minot. A farmer about a mile away, while walking from his barn to his house, having finished his chores late, saw the flash of the explosion and subsequent fire off in the distance. He jumped into his Model-T and headed down the road in the direction of the fire. Halfway there he was flagged down by a man in desperate need for help, some of his clothes burned off with blistered, oozing, peeling skin where the clothes had been. He begged the farmer to bring him to the hospital in Minot without delay, explaining he was driving down the road, lost after making a wrong turn on the way back to Minot from a pop delivery in Antler, and without warning his truck catching on fire, and the gas tank exploding. He had been thrown out of the cab of the truck, right through the right door of the cab, landing on the ground two rods away, where he lay stunned for some time before being able to get to his feet and stumble to the road the farmer found him on. After the farmer delivered the truck driver to the hospital, he visited the sheriff, thinking it best to report what he knew. The sheriff visited the scene the next day, finding himself puzzled by what he saw, a large amount of broken glass, some of the pieces being large enough to be identifiable as whisky bottles. He postponed talking to the Minot Pop Company man about it until he was taken off the critical list. The truck driver's explanation was he used old whisky bottles to store some of his pop syrups in. Unlikely, thought the sheriff, but he chose not to pursue the matter further. The poor man was suffering enough from the encounter in the dark of the night.

Clutch and the two men drove non-stop all way back to Janesville, trading off driving. They talked callously of the fate of the truck driver, assuming he was burned to death. This lack of concern for life by the two henchmen was understandable. Their upbringing on the streets of Chicago had hardened them. But how Clutch was able to shut down his emotions was more difficult to analyze. This was not the first time Clutch had hurt someone. He suffered night sweats and horrible dreams after his first violent commission. Then he did it again, and then again to where familiarity took over and it became routine, finding himself in denial and to be numb to the consequences of his acts. A double personality developed; one for his acts of violence, one for his love and kindness towards his friends and family. Both of them were verbally subdued people, not much talk but a lot of action.

CHAPTER EIGHT

Clutch visited Don Sigarto Bellagio the day after returning to Janesville. When Clutch had finished telling the story, the Don said, "Did the truck driver die? Clutch answered, "I am assuming he burned to death. Regardless, I am sure he will think twice before going back into the business of bootlegging whiskey from Canada." The Don said, "You probably can carry that a step further by saying; 'nor will anybody else in Minot consider it'. Clutch you do excellent work for me. I will reward you. My syndicate is going to expand further west, into Montana, Idaho and Wyoming. It is going to have to be done by railroad transportation. The distances are too great to cover by automobile. We will set it up like the operation run by Fiagio Corcione that now terminates at Valley City, North Dakota. I anticipate some trouble from a syndicate that now distributes whiskey out of Seattle, Washington, east into Montana, Wyoming and Idaho. They are mostly selling Canadian whiskey bootlegged in from the city of Victoria on Vancouver Island by high-powered speedboats. They do offer some European liquor smuggled into Seattle on ocean freighters. I know some of the leaders of the Seattle Syndicate and have communicated with them about our agreeing to limits to our prospective territories. I do not appreciate the way they are responding to my suggestions. I guess I will have to talk to them face to face, so I am planning a trip to Seattle next week. Will you travel with me? By the way, you are to be receiving a considerable raise in your salary starting this month. We will travel out on Milwaukee train # 29 to Prairie du Chein where we will transfer to the Great Northern Empire Builder, first class all the way." Clutch scratching his head, said, "Let me think about it ten seconds. Ten seconds up, YES! What day do we leave? Sig said, "A week from today, 10:00 AM, Janesville station, track #4. I am also bringing the same two men that traveled with you to Minot. I understand from them that the three of you got along well with each other."

Clutch spent the next week at his shop, interfering very little with the excellent job his manager was doing. Clutch had a long meeting with him one day, discussing some general policies. The meeting ended with Clutch telling the manager, as of that month, he would be giving him a large raise in his salary. Clutch made contact with all of the deliverymen in his district to make sure there were no problems with any of their customers or the law officers. He found everything to be running smoothly. The money was rolling in. Americans were enjoying the availability of liquor more and more, a pleasant repast for many. Society was claiming this as an inviolable right. Agitation for Repeal of Prohibition was becoming stronger and stronger. Sig and Clutch discussed this matter at great length during the long train ride. There was a wait between trains at Prairie du Chien. Sig and Clutch and the two henchmen visited the pool hall where the trouble had erupted a year before. The proprietor assured them that there had been no more problems. Apparently the solution to the earlier problem had discouraged any other customers from complaining and had discouraged any other lawyers from taking on the Syndicate or its customers. They had a nice lunch and a couple of beers with the proprietor. They also made a call on the Crawford County Sheriff at the county jail. He ushered Sig and Clutch into his office, the two henchmen waiting in the taxi. The sheriff asked if he could be of any help. Sig said, "We are just passing through and thought it would be nice to make a goodwill call." The conversation changed to duck hunting, which the sheriff said had been excellent on the backwaters of the Mississippi throughout late fall. Clutch told of his duck hunting in North Dakota. The sheriff invited Clutch to join him for a few days next fall. He had a hunting shack not too far out of town where they would stay overnight, Sig was welcome too, but he declined, duck hunting not being one of his interests. It was a pleasant visit. Sig announced to the sheriff on the way out that his next gift to the sheriff was going to be doubled. He didn't want the sheriff to be short of campaign funds for his next re-election. The sheriff thanked Sig graciously. They hugged, with Sig kissing the sheriff on both cheeks, Sicilian style. The sheriff was flattered.

The trip west on the Great Northern Empire Builder was comfortable, but long, four days and three nights. They had two compartments in a Pullman car, Sig and Clutch in one, the henchmen in the other, though they spent most of their time in the Club Car, where they were pleased to find highballs available if one slipped an extra 25 cents to the waiter. It was dinnertime shortly after they boarded. The front half of the Club car was the first class dinner. The fare was excellent, as was the service by the black waiters. All four men had rare beef au jus, thick slices, with au gratin potatoes, garden peas in cream and cherry pie. There was a poker game going in the club car after dinner, which all four men entered. The betting was too heavy for the two henchmen so they dropped out early. Clutch found himself holding his own. He dropped out fairly early also. Sig was a big winner, the game becoming a little rough in the late hours. He cleaned out several players. He was a master at gambling, never becoming too tired for more. He never rose for breakfast the next morning. The scenery across the northern plain states was rather monotonous. Nevertheless, Clutch found it interesting, seeing small farm place after small farm place, engaged in subsistence living, small towns trackside, barely surviving on the many promises made to them by Railroad Tycoon James J Hill, who was the namesake of the train that sped miles across the plains. Clutch had risen above the level of the struggling white settlers, always by honesty, though sometimes with violence. Clutch's ideation on the subject of his activities sometimes seemed to be running in circles, like a tiger chasing its tail, until he would convince himself that he was satisfied with the way he was.

Clutch had read of the Rocky Mountains, seen photographs and paintings of them, but never setting eyes on them. The third morning on the train the sky was clear but for a few cumulus clouds on the western horizon. The train had stopped to change crews at Havre, Montana, made a whistle stop at Shelby. Clutch knew the mountains should first come into view before the train reached the town of Cut Bank. Clutch pulled on his Harris Tweed topcoat with matching hat, wrapped a wool scarf around his neck, drew woolen gloves onto his hands and posted himself in the vestibule between the club car and the next car forward, his Pullman car, where he could open the window to give a better view west. Suddenly he saw them, glistening white peaks all along the horizon, covered with fresh snow of the early fall, his first view of the Rocky Mountains. It impassioned him, moved him to find Sig and the two henchmen to invite them to take a look. They were also fascinated. It was cold in the vestibule but tolerable to Clutch. He stayed there till the train pulled into East Glacier Station. The conductor announced a 20 to 30 minute wait while an extra engine was attached to the front of the train to assist in the climb over Marias Pass. During the delay, Clutch left the train to get some exercise by strolling up and down the station platform. He noticed the huge East Glacier Hotel only a block north of the station, now closed for the winter. This hotel, along with the entire chain of hotels and lodges in Glacier Park, some reached by bus, some only horseback or boat, were all owned by the Great Northern Railroad Company. An attractive summer vacation included transportation to the park, from either east or west, by railroad, then travel through the park by bus, boat, or horseback with stays at several hotels or lodges. There was no highway through the center of Glacier Park. Lake McDonald Hotel, located west of the continental divide, had to be reached by traversing Logan Pass on horseback or boating up Lake McDonald from its western end on the Launch DeSmet. Clutch was impressed with the laborious climb the train made up Marias Pass, even with the extra engine. The train stopped again briefly at the small village of Summit, while the extra engine was disconnected. There was a good depth of new snow on the ground at Summit, the elevation there being 5,280 feet. The next stop was at West Glacier Station, only two miles from the west end of Lake McDonald. Very few passengers got on or off these stops in the mountains, the rest of the day was spent circling north of the Salish Mountain Range through the northern most town of Eureka, south again to Libby, and at that town heading west again to cross into the state of Idaho, high mountain peaks towering over the route all afternoon, finally blanketed by nightfall at the State Border. It had been a day of unbelievable scenery. Clutch couldn't quit talking about it over cocktails in the club car, continuing the conversation over dinner at the diner. He was so fatigued that evening he excused himself from the poker game.

The next morning the four men were eating breakfast in the dining car while the train was being serviced in the train yard at Everett, Washington, just fifty miles north of Seattle. Clutch said to Sig, "Can you tell me a little about this man we are going to visit in Seattle?" Sig answered, "I'll tell you what I know. I met him one time in Chicago years ago his name is Ben O'Ryan. He is a loud-mouthed Irishman, who thinks he owns the world. He has met with some success with bootlegging in the Pacific Northwest. The chief of police of Seattle is also Irish. I have met and dealt with many fine Irish, honest, gentlemanly people, but these two men in Seattle are not known for these qualities. I have talked on the telephone to O'Ryan several times to reassure him I do not want to infringe on his territory, but I do want to establish a line between his area and mine. He refuses to make any commitments. I sense he has been drunk when we have talked. We will see. I have the address of his office. I suspect it is in the back room of a nightclub he owns near the waterfront on Puget Sound. I will telephone him after we have settled into our hotel. We are staying at the Chief Seattle Plaza, where I have reserved a suite of rooms. I hope O'Ryan will come there to visit us rather than us having to go to his office. There is an advantage in being on one's own turf.

The men took a taxi from the train station to the hotel. The first thing they all wanted was a tub bath after sponge bathing and spraying themselves with cologne for four days. Next they beckoned the hotel laundress to do up their underwear, socks and shirts and press their extra suits. Sig telephoned O'Ryan and invited him to join him in his suite for dinner. This put O'Ryan on the defensive but at the same time he didn't feel he could offend Sig by refusing the invitation. O'Ryan accepted his offer and would arrive for dinner at 8:00. Sig instructed Clutch and the two henchmen to place their belongings out of sight inside the closets. Sig felt it best that O'Ryan knew not that he had traveling companions. He further instructed Clutch and the two henchmen to eat out, attend a movie or two and not be back at the hotel until midnight.

Don Sigarto Bellgio received the Irishmen, Mr. Ben O'Ryan, with cordiality and some formality when he arrived at the hotel suite. It was apparent to the Don that Mr. O'Ryan had indulged himself prior to arrival, he being inappropriately affable and boorish for the occasion. Mr. O'Ryan slapped Don on the back with vigor, and said, "How are things, Sig?" Sig answered reservedly, "Fine, Ben, Fine, How have you been?" He responded, "A bit bilious at times, I feel my liver to be failing." With that self- appraisal of his health, Ben was offered some Port Wine by Sig. It had been delivered to the room after Sig had made an inquiry of the hotel Bell Captain at his stand in the lobby. The label on the bottle revealed it to have been imported from Portugal. Sig poured portions into two 3 oz. Port glasses, then raising his glass to Ben, offered a toast to Ben's good health. Their glasses clicked together. Ben threw his portion directly down his gullet. Sig rolled his portion in his glass, savoring the snifty aroma, before putting the glass to his lips for a small sip. Ben directly poured himself another portion, filling his glass to the brim. Sig decided he better get dinner on its way before this bore of a man ran the evening into the pits. Sig called room service, telling them to serve dinner promptly. Sig had ordered broiled lamb steak with a tomato/mushroom sauce over Spanish rice with fried seasoned zucchini as a vegetable, a bottle of white Zinfandel, imported from France, in the center of the table. The waiter stood inconspicuously, a discreet distance from the table. The dessert was Mardi Gras cake with caramel sauce, served with strong Arabian coffee. Sig dismissed the waiter. Ben had by now emptied the wine bottle, his speech becoming garbled. Sig said, "Ben, I am here in Seattle to talk to you about our same interests in bootlegging whiskey into the western states. I do not want our delivery people getting in each other's way. That would only result in competitive pricing, no good for either party. I have a map upon which I have drawn a proposed boundary. It runs through Billings, Montana, Casper, Wyoming and Denver, Colorado. Wouldn't this be agreeable to you?" Ben answered, "No, I am not going by any map. I will go where I want to, and you wont stop me." He was infuriated, appearing to lose control of himself. All graciousness was out the window. Ben stood up, nearly falling until he grasped the back of his chair, pulled the map off the table, ripping it in two, saying, as he had the pieces of the map to Sig, "There is a boundary for you." With that gesture he staggered out the door, grabbing for the door handle several times before getting it open, then slamming the door behind him as he left. Sig recognized that no further conversation would be of value. He went down to the hotel lobby to buy an evening newspaper, also to make sure Mr. O'Ryan wasn't hanging around. Sig hoped he had taken a cab from the hotel. Behind the steering wheel he would be a danger to any citizen on the street. Sig stayed in the hotel lobby til Clutch and the henchmen showed up. He didn't want to be alone with Ben O'Ryan on the loose.

When the men were in their suite, Sig told them of O'Ryans behavior. Sig said, "The man is a tempest. He is no good to anybody. I think I have the solution. Tomorrow I want you two men (speaking to the henchmen) to shadow him from his nightclub to where he spends his nights. I am assuming he has a home. I want to find out where it is and what time he returns to it for the night. Clutch, you and I have some chores of our own to perform."

First off the next morning, Sig and Clutch visited the Seattle dealership for Alfo Romeo Automobiles. The owner was a Sicilian. He and Sig hit it off like old home week. Sig asked if he could rent an automobile for a few days. The dealer said, "Of course, you can have any auto in the place." Sig picked out a large four-door sedan. Before leaving he asked the dealer if there were any construction firms in Seattle owned by Sicilians. The dealer said there was one. He gave the name to Sig. Sig and Clutch visited the firm's office and asked to see the owner. The owner was in a room adjoining the front of the office. He heard the request and recognized the accent of the man making it. The owner barged through the door of the room he was in, saying, I am the owner, I heard you talking, you have to be from Sicily. I am Sicilian myself, Elano Olciano, and proud of it, come on in. Clutch waited outside. Behind a closed door, Sig got to the point real quick, asking Mr.Ociano if he knew Mr. Ben O'Ryan. He said, "I do and have nothing good to say about him." Sig explained that the man needed to be done away with. That raised Mr. Olciano's eyebrows as he said, "Where do I come into this scheme?" Sig asked next if the firm was currently doing any concrete work. Elano told Sig they were nearly always doing concrete work, describing Sig a job they were on currently that was in operation twenty four hours a day. The job involved construction of concrete footings ten feet in diameter for a new building on the waterfront. Sig asked. "Elano, could you visit the site early in the morning, before sunrise, two days from now and call the men away from the site for a short meeting. Elano agreed, not asking any questions. Sig thanked Elano, then asked if the two of them could visit the site sometime tomorrow. Elano suggested 4:00 PM, to meet here at his office. Sig thanked him again, than left. Sig and Clutch drove by Mr. Oceano's construction site but could not get close to the work area. Sig explained his plan to Clutch, in vague terms, over lunch in the highest class Italian Restaurant in Seattle. It was 3:00 PM when they returned to the hotel, ready for a workout of swimming in the hotel's indoor, heated pool. Following that hour of pleasure, Sig and Clutch went for a long, brisk walk along the waterfront. It was a cold, sunless day, common during the fall and winter in Seattle. A mist hung over Puget Sound, the heavy air muffling the bass notes of the whistles of the phantom ships plying the waters. The high-pitched calls of they myriad seagulls were a constant song. The wharfs of the fisherman were bare of their ships, all out to sea, hauling in their catch to deliver to the fish market at daybreak the next morning. When they returned to the hotel, the two henchmen were lounging in the lobby, people watching. They, all four, went to their suite. The two henchmen informed Sig they had learned considerable about Ben O'Ryans habits of daily activity: "He arrives at his nightclub mid-afternoon, oversees its operation, getting further into the sauce every hour til he gets a taxi to take him home about 1:00 AM. Yes he has a home, in the hills about two miles east of downtown Seattle. The men had hired a taxi to take them past it. There is a long path from where the taxi lets him off to where he enters the house, which is poorly lit, the only street light being one half block away. He is not married, has no children. His long time girlfriend lives with him. She goes to bed about midnight." Sig asked, "Where did you two obtain all this information?" Their answer, "From the taxi driver. We are going to confirm these findings tonight." Sig said, "You will not need a taxi. We have a rented car you can use. Do not make yourselves to conspicuous. You need to park away from O'Ryan's nightclub. Do not spend time in the open near O'Ryan's house also park a long distance away.

Seclude yourselves well." Early that evening the four men went to the Palace Movie Theater. Harold Lloyd in "WELCOME DANGER" was showing. It was one of the first full length "talkies", a sound track of voice, music and sound effects. Prior to that all films had been "Silent Pictures", in which the voice script was printed on the bottom of the screen, the only sound being the piano player in the pit in front of the screen. Some large theaters had small orchestras instead of just a piano player. The music would fit the mood of the film. This new Harold Lloyd film, with the sound track, had been a sensation across the nation. Lloyd was a comedian who had been very popular in "Silent Films". The four men laughed through the entire film. After the movie they had a late dinner at a Chinese restaurant near the hotel, the menu was authentic Cantonese. There were no alcoholic beverages available in the restaurant, the Chinese preferring to stay clear of the law. The two henchmen took the Alfo Romeo from the restaurant. Sig and Clutch walked back to the hotel. After listening to a blaring, static filled radio in the lobby for a while they retired back to their suite and quickly to bed. They were tired. When the two henchmen came in about 2:30, they entered the suite through a separate door from the hall, directly into their bedroom, so as not to disturb Sig and Clutch. All four men slept late in the morning, then ate breakfast in the suite, to be able to discuss plans for the next night in private. The henchmen reported to Sig that O'Ryan had arrived at his home as predicted, by taxi, at 1:30 AM, so inebriated he could barely navigate the path into his house. In fact, he fell into a row of high bushes along the path, struggling for a time to get back on his feet. The taxi had driven off immediately after O'Ryan paid the cabby. Clutch drove Sig to the office of the Olciano Construction Company that afternoon to meet Mr. Olciano at 4:00 PM. Clutch waited outside in the Alfo Romeo. In a few minutes, Sig and Elano came out and climbed into Elano's ford truck and drove off. The visit to the construction site revealed the huge concrete pilings being built to support a multi-storied new building. The forms were metal, ten feet in diameter, thirty-five feet deep, networked with reinforcement rod. Ten of the pilings were completed. There were ten more in various stages of completion, one about one forth full of concrete, ready for additional filling during the coming night. It was located close to the gate where workers entered the construction area. Sig repeated the request to Elano that he had made previously, "Will you be able to visit the site at 5:30 AM, and call your workers away from their jobs into the windowless, construction site shack for a fifteen minute meeting. The workers may, preferably, leave the huge gas engine powered cement mixer running while they were at the meeting. One more thing, Elano; please leave the gate open when you enter the construction site." Sig noted that a long chute carried the mixed concrete from the mixer to the pilling form being filled. Elano volunteered that the chute would be directing concrete to the form located near the entrance gate early the next morning. It was also noted by Sig that no horizontal reinforcement rod had yet been placed in the upper portion of the form near the gate. Only a vertical rod was in place. Elano reassured Sig that would still be the case early the next morning. Additonal horizontal rod would not be placed until one more load of concrete was dumped into the form at 5:45AM, after the meeting with the workers, and until after that load of concrete had set. On the way back to the Olciano Construction Company office, Sig thanked Elano for his cooperation and generosity and asked him if he would accept delivery to his home in the near future of a case of the finest of French brandy. Elano thanked Sig graciously. Clutch was some relieved when Sig and Elano returned to the Construction Company office. It had been unusual for Sig to venture out without having at least one of his employees with him. One never knows.

When Sig and Clutch returned to the hotel, the two henchmen were in the suite. The four men had a short meeting. Sig reminded everyone there would be no consumption of alcohol tonight. It might be good for all of them to take a good swim in the indoor, heated hotel pool right now, before they went out to dinner, suggesting the Italian restaurant he and Clutch visited before was his preference. All agreed. Sig allowed ordering of one bottle of wine with the meal, served to them under the overhanging tablecloth. How can one enjoy an Italian meal without wine? It was near midnight when they finished dinner. Clutch got behind the steering wheel of the huge Alfo Romeo, Sig in the front passenger seat, the two henchmen in the back seat. They drove to the neighborhood where Mr. Ben O'Ryan resided. They surreptitiously drove the streets near O'Ryan's home. The area was devoid of any activity, no late parties, no barking dogs, no patrolling police cars, or insomniac night strollers. At 1:00 AM Clutch parked the Alfo Romeo around the corner from O'Ryan's house, car lights off, sitting for fifteen minutes in darkness to accommodate their vision. At 1:15 all four men put on their black hoods and patted the revolvers in their shoulder holsters. The two henchmen left the auto, walked around the corner and snuck up behind the hedge along the path from the street to O'Ryan's house. There they waited. As expected, a taxi drove up in front of O'Ryan's house at 1:30. It was obvious that O'Ryan was very inebriated. It took him several minutes to climb out of the taxi and several more minutes to pay the cabby. After the cab drove off O'Ryan stood at the beginning of the path as though he were some confused. Clutch had quietly moved the Alfo Romeo closer to the corner where he and Sig could bring O'Ryan into their view, leaving the engine running, quiet as a purring kitten. They saw O'Ryan slowly move up the path towards the house. Suddenly the two henchmen appeared from behind the hedge, one with a leather thong, crossed in his strong hands, which he quickly slung around O'Ryan's neck and tightened it to where not a noise was uttered from O'Ryan's throat. The other henchman grabbed O'Ryan at the waist. The two henchmen together threw O'Ryan to the ground; face down, the thong kept taught. Clutch quietly drove the Alfo Romeo up beside O'Ryan. The four men placed him on the floor of the back seat. He at first struggled some but soon became motionless. He was dead. The Alfo Romeo left the scene, undetected, in the dark of the night.

It would be more than three hours before they were due at the Olciano construction site. Sig had set the time of 5:30 AM for Elano to call his men into the construction site shack because a meeting at the earlier hour of 2:00AM would have aroused suspicion. So, what is there to do to pass time at 2:00AM on a cold foggy, rainy night in Seattle, Washington? It was Clutch who suggested, "Let's go down to the sound and watch fishing boats come in to unload their catch. They should be starting to arrive about this time." Clutch's suggestion was accepted. They had to park a quarter mile away. A lap robe was thrown over O'Ryan's body. A stretch of wharfs about one half mile long served as the berths for the boats. Behind the wharfs was a long empty space, which served as a fish market. Commercial buyers purchased a major portion of the catch, some agreements pre-agreed before the boats had gone out to sea. The major part of large purchases went to nearby canneries, whose boilers where steamed up, the factory crew prepared to clean the fresh salmon, cooked in the small cans to be distributed by rail to grocery stores throughout the nation. The fish came out of the ship's holds where they had been packed in chipped ice. The ship's crew sorted them by size, placed them in wooden crates, and then covered them with more ice chips. Fish for small purchaser, restaurants, rooming houses and housewives were displayed on tables, laden with more chipped ice, ready for sale in the morning. Fish sold to small purchasers commanded at a better price. The entire enterprise was a novelty to inlanders like Sig, Clutch and the two henchmen.

1929 DESOTO

At 5:00AM the men were headed to the Olciano construction site. The site was illuminated by gaslights. Clutch parked across the street from the gate, car lights off. It was noticed the gate was open. In but a few minutes, the workmen were seen to be heading for the construction site shack. A few minutes more and Clutch drove the Alfo Romeo through the gate up along the first piling form. The two henchmen dragged the body of O'Ryan out the back door of the auto and tossed it into the piling form. They had looked in when they heard a plop, seeing the body nearly buried in fresh concrete, then rubbed their hands together as a gesture of accomplishment in the dark of night. The henchmen jumped back into the car as Clutch was already turning around to drive out of the gate. Clutch parked across the street again where the piling form was still in view. Five minutes later the workmen came out of the shack, one going directly to the cement mixer, which had been mixing load concrete the entire time the men were in the shack. He tipped the mixer to dump its contents into the chute running to the pilling form where O'Ryan's body had just been thrown, now buried in concrete forever. Mission complete.

Clutch drove directly back to the hotel. The four men went right to bed, 'dead' tired. They slept till noon, packed their suitcases, had a bug lunch in the hotel restaurant, checked out of hotel, Sig paying their bill in cash. There was to be no evidence of their registration, for Sig had checked into the hotel with a false identification. They returned the Alfo Romeo to the dealership, Sig requesting the dealer to forget that the car had never been rented. They took a cab to the railroad station arriving in plenty of time for the departure of the eastbound, 3:00PM Great Northern Empire Builder. Sig bought a copy of the early issue of <u>THE SEATTLE EVENING TIMES</u> as they walked by the newsstand. A headline half way down the front page read: BEN O'RYAN, LOCAL BUSINESS MAN REPORTED MISSING. The story told of Mr.. O'Ryan's lady friend reporting to the Seattle Chief of Police at 9:00AM that her Ben had not come home last night as was always his custom. The police had located and interviewed the cab driver that had delivered Mr. O'Ryan to his home at 1:30AM. The cab driver stated he helped Mr. O'Ryan out of his cab and saw him heading down a path to the house as he drove away. Foul play is suspected. The cabby is not a suspect. The police investigation had, so far, found only one piece of evidence; tire marks of a heavy automobile on the front yard of Mr. O'Ryan's property. Mr. O'Ryan's lady friend was very distraught. Mr. O'Ryan had not told her of a confrontation he had recently with an out of town businessman, but had not identified him nor had Mr. O'Ryan disclosed the nature of the confrontation. The Chief of Police said, "I have no leads, I invite anyone that may have observed anything unusual of late, regards Mr. O'Ryan, to please telephone or visit my office. The investigation will remain open." Later when Sig and Clutch were enclosed in their Pullman car compartment, Sag's only comments were, "Even if they found out about us, even if they prosecuted us, they could never make conviction of murder without the body, and they will never find the body, thanks to Elano Olciano, and he will never talk. He understands "Omerta", the mafia code of silence.

He was born in Sicily, like myself. I predict we will remain good friends in the future."

The train ride back to Wisconsin was routine. There was no view of the Rocky Mountains. The area was heavily clouded. It was snowing all across the western part of Montana. The men gave up poker on the way back and took up the game of hearts. It was more to the liking of the two henchmen. When Sig and Clutch were together in their compartment, they talked a great deal about Clutch's future in the Syndicate. Sig wanted Clutch to sell **THE CLUTCH SHOP,** so Clutch could devote full time to the Bellagio Syndicate. Clutch did not think that was necessary. It was taking very little of his time anyway. Sig's concern was that if Clutch ever did get in trouble with Federal Agents the first thing they could do, would be to attach his assets, including **THE CLUTCH SHOP**. Sig said, "That would not happen to me. None of my property is in my name. The titles are all obscure." Clutch's answer was, "I'll take my chances." Sig's further discussion involved his plans to move further west, now that O'Ryan had been eliminated. He had previously promised Fiagio Corcione that he was going to take him off the train route to Valley City, North Dakota. Fig had a lovely wife and two children and deserved to not have to be away from home so much. Sig could now plan to locate Fig in Billings, Montana, putting some younger men with him, to do the traveling, and place the entire western operation under Fig. Clutch would assume supervision of the entire eastern operation; Wisconsin, Minnesota and the Dakota's. "Clutch, I gave you a raise a month ago, but now I will double that salary if you take over the Eastern operation." Clutch said, without hesitation, "I'll take it!" The men all did a lot of napping and eating on the train ride back to Wisconsin. Clutch and Sig walked to the station platforms whenever there was any stop over. Sig had practically kick the two henchmen off the train to join Clutch and himself. They were inherently lazy.

CHAPTER NINE

Back in Janesville there was excitement on every corner. The Roaring Twenties were roaring louder and louder. New businesses were flourishing everywhere. Wall Street was a frenzy. Millionaires were being made, one a minute. Increasing consumption of liquor walked arm in arm with affluence. **THE CLUTCH SHOP** was doing great. Clutch had to enlarge the building, purchase more equipment and hire more mechanics. He further raised the manager's salary. Clutch was putting away a lot of money, some in savings accounts, some in the stock market, some in cash in a big safety deposit box, some sent to his sister, Priscella, to do with what she wished. He bought a small dairy farm a few miles north of Janesville. A manager, farm hands, and dairymaids came with it. He paid cash, putting Priscella's name on the deed. It did not bring in much money but it was a solid investment and required nothing from Clutch but major policy decisions. The increasing demand for liquor further accelerated as more and more pool halls, dance pavilions and speakeasies came into existence. Clutch was to go to all of the time arranging terms to supply them with liquor. If the managers of these new establishments couldn't come to terms with the local law enforcement people, Clutch had to step in. His dealings with the sheriff's and police officers usually involved entertainment of the officers and their wives with subsequent payoffs to the officers and elaborate gifts to the wives, fur coats, refrigerators, cabinet radios, gift coupons to beauty studios, sets of sterling silverware and other gifts of equal worth, nothing cheap. Paying off the wives was more important that paying off the officers. The system worked, nearly to a flaw. Federal agents were different. It was difficult for them to accept bribes. They were never out in the open, instead constantly undercover, unidentifiable and incognito. The Bellagio Syndicate had a huge problem erupt over a shipment of liquor on a paddle wheeler out of New Orleans. The liquor shipment was packed tightly in a shipment of furniture from Italy. The Feds knew there were large supplies of liquor coming out of Joliet and were determined to find out the source. The Feds infiltrated the long shore man's union local list in Joliet, Illinois where the paddle wheeler was to be unloaded. A federal agent obtained a job as a long shore man, helped unload the shipment of furniture, helped unpack it at a warehouse where it was separated into the furniture imported from Italy arrived. Ten federal agents, with revolvers drawn, were hiding in the warehouse. Without a shot being fired, they were able to confiscate the liquor and the trucks, apprehend the Bellagio Syndicate's truck drivers and the long shore men crew. No one talked. Omerta held. Sigarto Bellagio hired the best lawyers in Chicago. The men all got off with small fine but the Syndicate lost its liquor and the use of the same route in the future. Sig developed a simple answer to the problem. The next shipment was taken off the paddle wheeler at Ottawa, Illinois, then shipped by train from there directly to a Chicago warehouse. The Feds never did figure out that scheme. The New Orleans part of the scheme had always been free of interference. The long shore man's union in New Orleans was so mean the Feds never dared enter the city, in fear of their lives.

The year 1928 enjoyed even higher economy that the previous years. The country was living on high. Janesville had two well-developed golf courses by this time, one a municipal course, one an exclusive Country Club. Clutch took some lessons the winter of 1928. He was surprised how well he enjoyed the swing of the golf club. The putting fascinated him to no end. Clutch's years of pool and billiards had sharpened his eye. He joined the Country Club. He was one of the first players on the course in the spring. He acquired a number of new friends. One young man in particular made it a point to play with Clutch. Clutch met several young ladies. He invited one to the Club's spring dance. Women were having as much fun as men in these high times with their bobbed hair, rouged cheeks, rolled down socks and short skirts. Clutch's feet were really loose that night, probably from sneaking out to his Austin/Healy in the parking lot for a shot of brandy several times. The feverishness of the Jazz Age was capturing his spirit. He dated the girl several more times but the relationship did not become serious. She was a terrible golfer. He preferred playing with men. He missed very few Men's days that summer and ended up playing in the club tournament, getting into the "second flight". He managed his work schedule to not conflict with his golf. On several occasions he entertained distant sheriffs, in his district, at the club, if they were enthusiasts of the game. Clutch carried his clubs in his auto, when he was away from Janesville and managed to find games with the customers of the syndicate at times. For the most part they were dedicated sportsmen.

F. Scott Fitzgerald, the twenty four year old Minnesota popular author, had caught the excitement of the razzle-dazzle 1920's in his novel, *This Side of Paradise.* Clutch had read it along with other Fitzgerald novels of the decade. Clutch, along with most others in America was having the time of his life. He sailed into 1929, flying high. TIME magazine of the first month of 1929 featured Walter P. Chrysler as the man of the year. He was building a brand of new skyscraper in Chicago and had introduced the new Plymouth and Desoto cars. Clutch gave up his beloved Austin/Healy, trading it in on a new Desoto, fitted with all of the extras available. Clutch had met up with a luscious red head. She was a female vocalist with a band playing regularly at a high-class dance hall on the shores of Lake Geneva, called the GENEVA BALLROOM. He had been there on New Years Eve with Sigarto Bellagio, Sigarto's wife and several other couples. They were all seated at the manager's special booth. Clutch inquired of the singer from the manager. He said she had been the girlfriend of the bands lead saxophonist, but it was his understanding that they had recently broken up. Clutch sent her a note asking her to join them at their booth at intermission. She accepted the invitation. She introduced herself as Sally Jo Young (real name- Sandra Youngstrom), a Swedish blonde, dyed red, the same age as Clutch. Their chemistries blended immediately. They danced during one of the numbers that didn't have singing lyrics. To Clutch it felt good to cling to a girl. It was his first female interest since dumping Josephine. Sally Jo responded to Clutch as though it felt good to her also. When the dance was over the two sauntered into the shadows of a setting of artificial palm trees and embraced each other seductively. Clutch was able to dance one more number with Sally Jo later in the evening. He came close to "making" her right on the dance floor. When the band left the stage at 1:00AM, Sig and his group moved to the lounge, Clutch and Sally Jo with them. It was obvious to everyone that Clutch and Sally Jo were really making out. When the party broke up at 3:00AM, Sally Jo asked Clutch to her apartment. He was staying at the Bellagios for the holiday and had ridden to the ballroom with them. He knew it would be improper to not ride home with them. He promised Sally Jo to return the next night with his own car. Clutch drove from Bellagios to the ballroom the next night, in spite of a raging blizzard. The ballroom was open, but there were very few guests. Clutch was able to signal Sally Jo from the edge of the dance floor that he was present. She joined him after her next vocal number. Clutch loved her voice, a deep contralto. He told her so. While they were sitting in the booth, Sally Jo's "Ex" walked by, remarking to her that he noticed she had latched on to a new chump. Clutch rose to his feet to offer a challenge but Sally Jo pulled him back down saying "Ignore him."

By 10:00PM there was not a dancer left on the floor. The storm had sent them all home. The band packed up. Clutch and Sally Jo moved to the dining room attached to the lounge, ordered a carafe of sparkling burgundy, and gazed into each others eyes, both of them with nothing on their minds but going to bed with each other. Clutch asked of her "Ex". Sally Jo said she had been trying to get rid of him for months. He had been drinking excessively. The leader of the band had warned him that he might lose his job. Sally Jo had warned him that he might lose her also. He had been living with her in her apartment. She booted him out, even having a lawyer obtain a stay order from the court to stop him from stalking her. It appeared to her that the bandleader was going to give her "Ex" his walking papers with his next pay envelope. Sally Jo's apartment was only a block from the ballroom. Actually it was the guest home of a large mansion on the lakeshore. They took Clutch's new Desoto. Sally Jo was impressed with it, as she did not have a car. There was no mistaking their intentions for the night. Clutch had bought a pack of Trojan condoms at a local drugstore. Right after the two arrived at the apartment Sally Jo donned a flimsy nightgown. Clutch removed his suit coat, shirt and undershirt. Sally Jo put a record of the "Blues" singing on her Victrola and dimmed the lights to that of one small table lamp. As Sally Jo flopped on the couch, Clutch untied the belt on her gown. She had nothing on underneath. As she slid over to make room for Clutch, the gown fell aside exposing her lovely, amply full breasts. Her body was lithe, not skinny, not plump. Her facial features were Grecian, well angled, even some abrupt denoting her Swedish ancestry. Her lips were full, sensuous, as Clutch had already found out. How inviting she was. Clutch stared into her eyes, intentionally prolonging his gaze until Sally Jo softly took a hold of his head, bringing it to her till their lips met, staying in contact for many minutes. Clutch then rose up, removing his trousers and underpants. Her gown had become further parted, exposing her lower body and thighs. Clutch lay back down on Sally Jo, his firm penis between her thighs. They kissed again, prolonging this foreplay ecstatically. Clutch cupped Sally Jo's breasts in both his hands. The nipples erected. He kissed both breast several times. Sally Jo murmured, "Clutch, I love your hands and lips on my body." She placed one of his hands on her pubic area. He placed one of hers on his penis. They kissed again in rhapsody. Clutch's penis penetrated Sally Jo's vagina. They were both experienced lovers. They knew they were ready to consummate their love. Sally Jo said, "Lets move to the bedroom". She threw off her gown. Clutch watched her walk gracefully from the living room, his hunger yet to be satiated. She first visited the bathroom, and then crawled under the sheets of her bed. Clutch took a Trojan from the pocket of his suit coat. He visited the bathroom where he carefully applied it to his penis. He did not want it to slip off with the chance of pregnancy on his hands. The two engaged in some more foreplay. Shortly after linking they reached orgasm, falling to sleep in copulation. The next morning they awakened to repeat their performance, not as early spent as the night before. They fell back to sleep for several hours then arose and showered. Sally Jo fixed a breakfast of eggs and fried ham, Clutch asking if she was trying to rejuvinate him.

Clutch visited the Lake Geneva Ballroom several times a week that winter, staying overnight with Sally Jo on each occasion. One Saturday night while he was waiting for Sally Jo to complete her stand he was approached by one of the waiters with a piece of note paper. It said, "Please come out by your car, someone wants to talk to you". Clutch responded, but as he left the ballroom he took his revolver from his armpit holster. He always carried it. He approached the location of his car gingerly, circling around the parking lot to come up from behind. As he snuck close to the car he saw what appeared to be Sally Jo's "Ex" standing in the shadows. Whoever it was had a pistol in his hand resting it on top of the car, pointing it in the direction of the ballroom. Clutch tiptoed up behind the man, put a half-nelson around his neck, knocking the pistol from his hand, throwing the man to the ground, where he could see it was Sally Jo's 'Ex'. Clutch leveled his revolver at the man's head, putting three shots right between his eyes, three shots in the dark of night, no witnesses. He had a gun silencer so there had been no report of its firing. Clutch opened the trunk of his Desoto, put the body in, being careful to avoid getting any blood on his own clothes. He threw the man's pistol in on top of the body and latched the trunk. When he re-entered the ballroom he located the waiter who had passed him a note, slipped a hundred dollar bill into his hand and told him to never mention the "note" to anyone if he valued his life. Clutch stayed over with Sally Jo that night, performing with more virility than ever and sleeping soundly after. He had previously suspected the sanity of Sally Jo's 'Ex'. The man was subsequently reported missing with no clues to his whereabouts. Clutch had several of his delivery men in Janesville bury the body deep in a wooded area north of town and also had them wash out the trunk of his Desoto. Case closed.

CHAPTER TEN

The Clutch/Sally Jo love trysts continued all summer. Clutch bought an inboard speedboat, the best Chris Craft available with a Chrysler marine engine, keeping it in a boathouse on the property where Sally Jo rented her cottage. The couple enjoyed the outdoor life, both polished their swimming ability, bought a surf board, made friends with several other couples, ate and drank in the best of speakeasies, became the best of ballroom dancers, literally "had a ball." Clutch kept at his golf but it did not enamor Sally Jo. Clutch preferred it that way. His interest was playing with his male friends and usually beating them. The news from Wall Street was the talk of the town that summer. Shoeshine boys were becoming millionaires over night with $100 investments. Clutch bought a few stocks, not heavily. He preferred material things. He sent a few thousand dollars to his father and Priscella, telling them to buy land, including himself as a co-owner. Land prices had skidded to new lows in the Dakotas that summer. Corn had become worthless, 3 cents a bushel. It was being burned as fuel rather than sold on the market. This was an ominous cloud on the horizon. President Hoover, from his office in the White House, could not read the signs. He was as surprised as anyone when at exactly 10:00AM, Thursay, October 24th, 1929, the gong of the New York Stock Exchange sounded. Stocks were plunging 10 points and more between transactions. Panic was spreading. Soon the floor of the Exchange was filled with milling, screaming men, there faces alabaster white with fear. The day would be known as "Black Thursday", the day the bubble of American prosperity burst. The economy had become bloated like an over inflated balloon ready to burst. Anyone predicting the "crash" had been labeled an alarmist. The "crash" was headlines in the newspapers of every major city in the USA.

By the end of the year 1929, the entire American economy had followed the stock market into ruin. Clutch noted a huge drop off in business at his Auto shop. The Bellagio Syndicate experienced a huge drop off in the demand for liquor, but business held up better than at Clutch's shop. He got rid of the shop, practically giving it away to his long time manager. This allowed him to concentrate on his job with Sig. The joblessness and the hunger for a little extra income by the man on the street brought many incompetents into the trade. Sig was determined to get rid of them, before the matter got out of control. This meant wiping out a few vulnerable bootleggers that were not a part of the Bellagio Syndicate and also meant lighting a hotter fire under the law enforcement people who were turning their backs on the small timers. Two extra henchmen were assigned to Clutch. Clutch would contact the intractable violators, making it clear to them to stop their bootlegging or pay the final penalty. The all pleaded poverty. Clutch did not hear them. Those that persisted in their trade were subjected to some sort of damage, which usually took the form of their car being set on fire or their stock of liquor being destroyed. If that didn't convince them to cease and desist, they would disappear in the dark of the night sometimes leaving grieving wives and children. No one would have the guts to try and replace them. Sheriffs who were not fulfilling their commitments to the Bellagio Syndicate were usually invited out to dinner by Clutch. During the course of the evening they were reminded of their obligations and why they were being so well compensated. If they appeared repentant, their wife usually received a mink fur coat within the next week. If the sheriff in question acted difficult or took the notion he was going to reform his county, he soon found out he was taking his life into his own hands. He was given one chance to reconsider, which they all did, except one. He was a newly elected sheriff in the far northern Minnesota county of Koochiching. He had ousted the long time lenient sheriff on a reformist campaign. Many splinter religious groups had supported him in his victory.

Clutch and his two henchmen visited the new Koochiching County Sheriff at the courthouse in International Falls, Minnesota shortly after he took office. He was recalcitrant to the receipt of any bribe money, actually becoming belligerent and threatening. He informed Clutch that the two speakeasies in International Falls and the one dance hall in south International Falls were going to be closed up as soon as he could obtain some help from the County Attorney. Clutch and his two henchmen visited with the County Attorney that evening over drinks at one of the speakeasies. He was much more amicable. After Clutch slipped him five $100 bills under the table he became downright cooperative. He said that he doubted if the sheriff had enough evidence on any of the establishments to bring action to against the owners. He further said it would take a bold late night armed raid to disclose the illegal activity of either of the two speakeasies or the dance ballroom. He doubted if the sheriff had that much guts. That was an underestimate. About one week after Clutch had visited International Falls, the sheriff and two of his deputies showed up at the ballroom on a Saturday night, demanding access. They bungled the whole operation. The owner demanded a search warrant, which they did not possess. They tried to find the District Judge and could not locate him. It turned out he was actually at the dance hall with his wife and another couple. The owner of the dance hall telephoned Clutch on Monday morning. Clutch talked to Don Sigarto Bellagio. Sig said, "Considering the size of the Syndicate's business in Koochiching County, we should not do anything, but letting one sheriff get by with misbehavior is just going to fortify the bravery of other nearby law enforcement officers. We cannot let that happen, punish him, Clutch." That was the end of the telephone conversation.

CHAPTER ELEVEN

Clutch and his two henchmen left for International Falls that afternoon, staying in Saint Cloud over night. They were in International Falls by late afternoon the next day. At the time of their previous visit they had found out where the sheriff's home was, a few miles west of the city, but at that time he had not scouted it. This was a must now. They drove to it before going into the city. They had also found out during their previous visit to "The Falls" that the sheriff had herd of purebred quarter horses including two very high priced stallions, which were his pride and joy. It was his pride and joy. It was dusk when Clutch drove past the sheriff's ranch. The major pasture was surrounded by a shelterbelt of coniferous trees. The herd in that pasture had access to a barn near the ranch house. It was further noticed that two of the horses were segregated in a small pasture with only a lean-to for shelter. These had to be the stallions. This smaller pasture was right next to the road, as though the sheriff wanted them to be visible to the public, his pride. Clutch slowed down his Desoto as he drove by the two stallions. They immediately came to the fence, hanging their heads over the top wire. Like horses will be, they were curious. Clutch drove on. The house was secreted behind the trees. No one could have possibly seen them drive by. Clutch took a different route back east to the city. They stayed in the South Side Motel that night, eating dinner at The Falls Restaurant after visiting the Downtown Billiard Hall where they downed a couple of shots of Canadian Club. Clutch invited the manager of the place to join them for their "bumps". Clutch asked him outright from where he obtained the Canadian Club. He insisted he bought all of his liquor from the syndicate. Clutch reminded him that choice was the only guarantee of protection from the new sheriff.

Clutch and the two henchmen left the motel at 4:00AM the next morning, drove directly out of town on the road past the sheriff's ranch, proceeding slowly, head lights off, dim road lights on, quietly stopping by the stallion's coral. The horses immediately came to the fence. The windows on the right side of the Desoto were rolled down. Clutch shined a 10-cell flashlight into the horse's eyes. They remained motionless. The two henchmen each picked up a semi-automatic Winchester 30-06, with silencers, off the floor by their feet. The henchmen in the right front seat took aim at the stallion on the left; the henchmen in the right rear seat took aim at the one on the right. By previous arrangement, Clutch said, "1,2,3, fire". The henchmen pulled their triggers, striking the stallions between the eyes. The two stallions quietly dropped to the ground, without even a gurgle. Clutch exited his side of the Desoto, with hammer, nail and a printed note. The note said, "IF YOU DO NOT LEAVE THE SPEAKEASIES AND BALLROOM ALONE, YOU MAY BE NEXT". Clutch nailed it to the closest wooden fence post. He climbed back into the Desoto, did a slow bootlegger's turn and quietly drove back down the road. They had left no evidence. The empty cartridges had fallen inside the car. Clutch had handled the note with gloves on. There were no tire tracks left on the road, in the dark of the night. The three men drove south that morning, stopping over night at Manhattan Beach Lodge near Cross Lake, Minnesota, attractive to the underworld for its famous gaming room in the basement of the lodge.

Next morning when the sheriff came upon the scene, he stood shaking and sobbing over his beloved horses. His remorse then quickly turned to anger. "I'll get those *sons of bitches"!* He telephoned his deputy to come to the ranch. The two scoured the area for evidence. They found none. The sheriff said, "I'll have the ballroom and the speakeasies closed by nightfall". The deputy told him to read the note again and advised caution. He told the sheriff to let well enough alone. The sheriff grumbled and swore then went to the house and telephoned the rendering plant.

CHAPTER TWELEVE

The winter had been long and cold. Unemployment lines in Janesville were lengthening every day. President Hoover was accomplishing nothing from the White House. The democrats were picking up steam. 1930 promised to make the poor poorer and the rich richer. Clutch and Sally Jo had Clutch's Chris Craft on Lake Geneva as soon as the ice was out. Clutch started hitting golf balls as soon as the snow was melted. Priscella wrote from home in North Dakota quite often. Clutch was not as good about answering. The big news this spring of 1930 was the announcement that Jeanie was going to be married on the 18th of June. She was 20 years old. She had attended high school in Voltaire where she received her diploma. Her fiancée was two years her senior. Jeanie had met him in high school. He had, ever since graduation, worked at the general store in Voltaire. Clutch sent Priscella $500 telling her to spend whatever was needed to give Jeanie the best wedding ever, flowers galore, a big reception at the church with a full dinner, dresses for the bridesmaids, a big dance that evening at the Voltaire Dance Hall with the High Hatters for a band, all ten pieces, to include piano and a female vocalist. Clutch wrote he was going to bring his better half. They could stay at his parents. He planned to arrive one week ahead of the wedding and stay at least one week after. He and Sally Jo drove the Desoto. They stopped at the Leamington Hotel in Minneapolis the first night. They had a deluxe room with breakfast in bed. They arrived at the Doyer's farmhouse late afternoon. Ann had a big dinner in the making with the guests already on hand; Priscella and her family, Papa Lee, Jeanie and her fiancée, Mary, Amy, Kim and Helen. Shane had been working on a ranch in Montana for several years. Winston had left that spring to join him. A huge ham was roasting in the oven. White rice, fresh green garden peas, leaf lettuce with fresh chives, fresh radishes and fresh baked rolls made it a feast. Fresh rhubarb pie topped with whipped cream was served for dessert. Sally Jo was impressed. Things were tough throughout the farm country. Thank heavens Lee Doyer owned all his land free and clear. They all had plenty of food but not much cash left over for purchase of any luxuries. Lee used his John Deere Model D sparingly. Gasoline had not dropped in price like corn and wheat had. Butterfat was their best money maker. Eggs had also remained at a reasonable price.

Everyone assumed Jim and Sally Jo were married. They slept together which otherwise would have been unheard of in rural North Dakota. Jim helped his dad with haying for several days and pitched into the milking twice a day. The girls helped also. Sally Jo fit in well, enjoying Ann and Priscella, spending time helping with arrangements for the wedding. She drove to the field with lemonade for the haying crew on several occasions. She made it clear to Jim that she was having the time of her life. Even calling him Jim instead of Clutch seemed to fit.

The June 18th wedding day delivered ideal weather, a shower in the morning to freshen the earth, sunshine in the afternoon to brighten the festivities. The church was packed. Everyone stayed for dinner and the cooks were prepared. Meatballs, mashed potatoes, brown gravy, fresh garden peas, fresh lettuce salad with radishes and table onions, rolls and coffee, milk and lemonade, all served by the girls of the congregation. Fresh rhubarb pie and ice cream were served for dessert. Favors were by every place, hatpins for the ladies, tiepins for the men, tin whistles for the children. The cooks were all given lovely kerchiefs. Garden flower arrangements were displayed on every table. Crape paper streamers hung from the ceiling. All the men were invited to Doyer's barn for drinks before the dance. Jim had brought the best of brandy and bourbon from Wisconsin. Jim was toasted several times with, "He's A Jolly Good Fellow." Jim glowed.

The dance was gay and loud. The bride and groom kissed so much their lips were sore. The bride had so many dollar bills pinned to her gown it nearly drug it to the floor. The men that had visited Doyer's barn were limber and flirtatious. But it was all in good fun. The band played till 2:00AM. A local piano player took over for two more hours. The light of the next day was showing in the east when the last man left the dance hall. Jim had given Jeanie and her new husband a hundred dollar bill and the use of his Desoto and told them to drive to Minot and stay in the hotel. Jeanie thanked Jim over and over. Everyone slept late Sunday morning, except the cows. They were up from the pasture, bellowing at the barn gate at 6:00AM, wanting to be milked. They were all fresh from calves, udders painfully swollen with abundant milk. Lee finally rolled out of bed at 7:00AM. No one else got up but him.

Clutch and Sally Jo stayed until the following Friday. There were many kitchen table meetings about this Great Depression. Who was this Franklin Roosevelt they were hearing about. Father Coughlin, the radical catholic priest in Detroit was attracting listeners to his nationally syndicated radio program. He threw support to Roosevelt. It was two years till the next national election but it could just as well been tomorrow. The country was fed up with President Hoover and his republican party. Only those who benefited from the many land foreclosures supported the republicans. Many farms were being abandoned. New owners by receivership could find no one to farm additional land. Drought added another dismal aspect. Dust storms swept fields bare, leaving very little grain to harvest. The rural scene was ghostly. It tore at Jim's heartstrings to leave his family in such an atmosphere of desperate survival. Some farmers were heading west. A few jobs were to be found in California. Novelist John Steinbeck's, *Pastures of Heaven*, told it all.

CHAPTER THIRTEEN

The rest of the summer of 1930 was mostly playtime for Clutch. Sally Jo gave up singing with the band. Her voice was becoming husky from her long hours at the microphone. Clutch was becoming frustrated by her late hours on the bandstand. They both kept their separate apartments, but Sally Jo started spending more and more time with Clutch in his Janesville place. The arrangement worked well, a place in town and a place at the lake. They developed new friends, mostly couples in the high social strata at Lake Geneva. Generous use of alcohol was part of their lives. Inebriation, though, was never their goal. Clutch always maintained control of his drinking. Sally Jo carried her drinking some further than Clutch at times. Clutch did not like her doing so, he scolded her.

That fall in October, Clutch went to Northern Wisconsin with three of his friends for a duck-hunting outing. They left on a Thursday, scheduled to be back in Janesville on Sunday. It was a private club owned by friends of Don Sigarto Bellagio from Chicago. They knew how to live as classy sportsmen. The facilities were plush, with guides, boats, decoys all furnished. Each day started with a big breakfast. Snacks and coffee were furnished in the blinds. Dinner was by a chef, roast duck with wild rice the first night in camp. Liquor was available in the lodge but not in the blinds. That Saturday night, the telephone in the lodge rang at 2:00AM. One of the guides had been to town and had just come in the back door. He answered the phone. It was Don Sigarto Bellagio. He wanted to talk to Clutch. Sig had a hard time getting out words. He was sobbing, finally Clutch understood him to say, "Sally Jo, had been killed in an automobile accident about 11:00PM, driving from Lake Geneva to Janesville." She and friends had been drinking at the Lake Geneva Supper Club that evening. She was determined to drive to Janesville late to be sure and be there when Clutch arrived home the next day. Her friends knew how much she had been drinking and tried to discourage her, to no avail. Her car went off the road just north of the town of Darien, striking a tree head on. Another driver, in the car directly behind Sally Jo, witnessed the accident. She had probably fallen asleep at the wheel. The other driver stopped, went directly to Sally Jo's car, finding no sign of life in her crumpled body. The body was now in the funeral parlor at Darien. Clutch sat by the phone for some time before awakening his friends. He was sobbing, his handkerchief wet with tears. His friends insisted that their stay at the lodge be cut short and that they all leave immediately for Janesville. It was mid-afternoon before they arrived home. Sig in the mean time had telephoned Sally Jo's family in Milwaukee. They had indicated that it would be their preference to have her funeral in their church with burial in the adjoining cemetery. Sig said he would convey their wishes to Clutch. When Sig told Clutch of the wishes of Sally Jo's family, he agreed to their plan. The funeral was set for the following Wednesday afternoon. Clutch had Sally Jo's body moved to a funeral home in Janesville that had a superb reputation for preparing the remains. He telephoned Priscella the next day. She called back within the hour telling Clutch she and Ann were coming to the funeral, taking the train directly to Milwaukee. They acquired a fondness for Sally Jo that spring and felt a kin to her. Clutch told her to buy first class tickets and a Pullman compartment. He would pay the costs. He also said he would make reservations for them at the Hoffman Hotel in Milwaukee where he was staying.   Clutch was extremely despondent the next few days. He involved his mind in a deep reevaluation of his life, questioning where it was leading him.   He spent Monday with the Bellagios at their home on Lake Geneva. A large number of cars drove from there to Milwaukee on Tuesday. Several friends of Sally Jo and Clutch's rode with Clutch in his Desoto, all staying at the Hoffman Hotel. Clutch and one of his friends met Priscella and Ann at the depot. The two ladies comforted Clutch lovingly. He sobbed uncontrollably when he first hugged them but then gained control of his emotions. The church was a parish of the Wisconsin German Lutheran Synod, an impressive edifice on an oak tree shaded residential street. The tree leaves were falling like a myriad of small parachutes on the day of the funeral. It had frozen hard the night before. The sun was shining brightly, creating a very heavenly setting as mourners entered the church sanctuary for the 10:00AM service. The church became filled with friends and relatives of Sally Jo's family and the friends from Lake Geneva. It amazed Clutch how many of the employees from the Bellagio Syndicate, with wives and girlfriends, had driven to Milwaukee for the funeral, all familiar to Clutch, some not having ever met Sally Jo. The front of the church was full of flowers. The casket, arranged for by Clutch, was beautifully carved black walnut. Sally Jo's parents who were of modest means could not have afforded such a rich casket. Her father being a brew master at the Schmidt's Brewery, which, of course was limited to the brewing of only "near beer" during prohibition. The casket was open for viewing prior to the service. Sally Jo was stunningly beautiful, even in death. The service was short, accentuated by an enchanting soprano solo given by a friend of Sally Jo's. The two had been members of a trio who entertained at speakeasies in Milwaukee a few years previously. The burial was at Lakeside Cemetery on the shore of Lake Michigan. It was such a calm sunshiny day. The lake was like glass, taking on the deep azure blue of the heavens above. Clutch sobbed, shoulders shaking, throughout the graveside ceremony. The tragedy had softened Clutch. He was entertaining the thought of taking his own life to join Sally Jo in heaven. His agnosticism, however, prevented him from believing this could happen. He was a non-believer of either heaven or hell.

A delicious lunch was served at a reception in the church hall after the funeral. It was prepared and served by one of the church circles. Clutch paid for it, giving the circle a very generous gift in addition to the cost of the lunch. Priscella and Ann stayed over that night in Milwaukee. They did not want Clutch to be alone. Clutch calmed down and talked about himself that evening over dinner. He was in a quandary about what to do with his future. He unveiled the secret about his job with The Don Sigarto Bellagio. Ann did not seem to be surprised. Priscella knew. There had been telltale signs, starting with the availability of liquor that seemed to be Clutch's good fortune and the character of the people from Janesville and Lake Geneva that attended Sally Jo's funeral. Before the evening was over he indicated to Priscella and Ann that he would stay in Janesville for the time being. The money was too much to give up quickly. He did know, however, that the opportunities for bootlegging were in jeopardy with the rising interest in repeal of prohibition. He also discussed with Priscella and Ann the changes that could be expected to occur if Franklin Roosevelt won the presidential election coming up in two years. Clutch promised to keep the family appraised of his plans. He further promised that they could plan on his being at the farm near Voltaire for Christmas. That was certain. He likely would stay a month, maybe more. They should plan on the biggest Christmas ever and a wild new years eve. His final word to the ladies at the train depot the next morning was, "Tell Lee not to be discouraged about the economy. Things will eventually improve."

Clutch spent a lot of time at the Bellagio Estate on Lake Geneva. Clutch had first thought he would keep Sally Jo's apartment at the lake, but gave up that bad idea, too many memories. Sig seemed to enjoy having Clutch around and Clutch enjoyed the company of Sig and his family. Much of their conversation revolved around the business of the Syndicate. It was holding up amazingly well, but Sig knew what would happen if prohibition was repealed. He talked of retiring to Sicily. He had enough in the way of assets secreted there to live very comfortably. On the other hand he preferred to have his children remain in the United States, principally to pursue a higher education if they were so inclined. He wasn't ready to make a decision yet. Neither was Clutch ready to make his decision. Clutch drove to Milwaukee every Sunday to visit Sally Jo's grave. He placed a dozen fresh red roses on the grave each time, no matter what the weather. He stood by the grave, his breast filled with heaviness and tears coming to his eyes. He would look up to the bare trees overhead, snowflakes melting on his warm face if it was snowing, sunshine striking his eyes if the sky was clear. The cemetery was a quiet place, a place to reminisce about all the good times he had with Sally Jo, their deep love for each other, how his life had been emptied by her sudden death. Several Sundays he attended the church where Sally Jo's funeral had been, sat with her parents, and then took them out for dinner after the service. They were grateful to Clutch for this kindness. Clutch always put a good size bill in the collection plate. This pleased the minister.

CHAPTER FOURTEEN

Clutch decided to drive the Desoto to North Dakota for Christmas rather than take the train. He did not want to be without transportation at Voltaire. He stopped in Minneapolis at the Leamington overnight. He did not stop in Valley City. He was not in the mood for that type of visit. It was late evening when he reached the farm. They were all up waiting for him, some concerned about the late hour of his arrival. The entire family individually offered their sympathies for the death of Sally Jo. He disclosed his miserable lonesomeness without hesitation, told them of his visits to Sally Jo's gravesite. Ann served a midnight snack of hot beef sandwiches, with cranberry jello, and chilled fresh milk. Jim asked Lee, "How many cows are you milking?" Lee said. "Twenty." Jim promised to get up and help him in the morning. Time now to go to bed.

Jim was up before Lee the next morning. The fire in the kitchen range had gone out overnight. Jim started it with a few corncobs, added some coal and put the coffee pot on. The fire in the basement furnace needed stoking. Jim took care of that. Lee was up by then, near 5:00AM. He had a quick cup of coffee with Jim before the two of them went to the barn. A covering of new fluffy snow had fallen during the night. There was no wind. Thin clouds were breaking up. A full moon was shining through the lingering lace of the white cirrus formation. It was so quiet, it was not heard, but felt. There was no sound. The soft snow underneath the boots of the two men dampened even the crepitation of their footsteps. It was peaceful quietness. It was soothing to Jim. He had not felt so relaxed since the first news of Sally Jo's accident. As the two men reached the barn, Lee stopped, turned around, looked back at the house, the kitchen window aglow from the Coleman gas lamp they had left burning, saying to Jim, "My it's a beautiful morning." Jim turned around too, looking skyward as he spoke, "Dad you are so right. I had felt it too."

Milking time is a time for milking partners to talk, to talk over serious matters. Each person is more or less hidden from the other person, alongside their respective cows, the seclusion resembling the confessional in the Catholic Church. The confessionist not having to look the listener in the eyes makes it easier for him to talk, particularly about sensitive topics. Lee started the conversation, "Jim, it must be very difficult with Sally Jo gone. She was a jewel among women. You had to be very much in love with her." Jim didn't have an immediate response. Lee waited patiently. Jim had moved to the next cow before saying, "Dad, I am sure you know how it is, having lost mother, like you did... It is tough, real tough. I cried my eyes out for weeks. It will help me to be here on the farm with you and the family. Ann is a wonderful lady. You should be proud you have her. Of course, I can't say enough good about Priscella. It meant a great deal to me for the two of them to travel to Milwaukee for the funeral. I do not know what I would have done without them to comfort me. Now my problem is: What should I do with my life? I haven't decided yet. Down deep I think I should make a change. The United States is changing. I should be changing with it. Prohibition will most likely be repealed. People enjoy the availability of liquor. Repeal would probably put and end to my job. Even though it has required being brutal at times, the work has been exciting and rewarding. I have no regrets about doing what I have done. What with the terrible economic insecurity throughout the entire world, it is not easy to pull up roots and replant oneself. I am left terribly undecided." Lee said, "My only help to you will be to let you talk about it. I am here for that. It will eventually work out. In the meantime I do not look down on you for the type of work you have been in. Ann tells me she met your boss, Sig, and his family at the funeral and was impressed with their quality. They were not a bunch of bums.

Ann had breakfast ready when Lee and Jim returned to the house after milking. Four of the children were still living at home, Kim and Helen still in country school, Mary and Amy riding the bus to Voltaire High School. Lee had hitched up the horse to a sleigh when he was done milking. He always chose a Queen for this job. She was old, obedient and gentle. Kim and Helen were capable of taking the sleigh to their school. They picked up the seven year old Hansen girl at her farm one half mile north of the Doyer place, saving her father from making the trip to school. There was a huge, heavy cow robe in the sleigh. The girls wrapped it around their legs and feet and across their laps, tucking their mitten covered hands under the robe and pulling their wool scarves up high on their faces, leaving only their eyes exposed.   Vision and control of the reigns were not necessary, the horse knowing the way well. Queen was allowed to trot with the sleigh, but it was against the rules to gallop. A hard snowdrift could upset the sleigh in a hurry. There was a barn behind the school, open on the south side with stalls for eight horses. A second story haymow was filled each fall. The children threw down some hay for their horses to munch on during the school day. A can full of oats from a bag on the back of the sleigh was thrown into the feed box at the head of the stall. If the girls neglected the oats, Queen let them know with a loud whinny. The system saved the parents having to drive back and forth to school twice a day. Kim and Helen loved Queen and Queen loved them. At times there would be a storm howling across the prairie. If it was too bad the girls stayed home. If it was of moderate severity, Lee hitched up his huskiest team to the dray sleigh and brought the girls to school.   If a storm came up unexpectedly during the school day, Lee would saddle up his riding horse, Prince and gallop down the road to the school, guiding the girls and Queen home. In the fall and spring, Queen was hitched up to a buggy. Neighbors once reported to Lee and Ann that they had seen Kim and Helen put Queen into a gallop for short distances. A talking to the girls stopped that. The only other choice was to walk to school.

Jim, Lee and Ann sat at the kitchen table long after breakfast that morning, talking mainly about Sally Jo's tragic death. Jim carried heavy guilt, feeling the high living he had enabled for Sally Jo was a big factor in the cause of her death. He could not shake this out of his mind. Lee and Ann tried to talk Jim out of his train of thought. It was no use. He said, "I only wish I could bring Sally Jo back. Things would be different." Ann said, "Jim, that will never happen."

Jim decided to drive to Minot that day, just to look around. He invited Lee and Ann to go with him, but they sensed he needed to be alone. There were three bowling alleys in town, one large one, two smaller ones. He visited all three, bowling several lines in each. He had done some bowling in Janesville the past years. He had a good skill for the game, as with other sports. He bowled alone. One man asked Jim to join him. Jim declined. Jim visited a long time with the owner of the large alley. The facility had three billiard tables and a small restaurant along with fifteen alleys. The owner was quite old. He indicated he would like to start spending less time in his business. Jim nodded his head. Later in the afternoon, Jim looked up the local representative of the Bellagio Syndicate. He found him to be a sick man, having recently been confined to the hospital, now home but not getting outside. Jim noticed the man had a yellow complexion, had an odor of alcohol on his breath and appeared to have lost a lot of weight. The man's wife whispered to Jim when he was putting on his overshoes in the front hall that her husband was dying from cirrhosis of the liver. He had been a chronic alcoholic for years. Jim's findings that day put him to doing some heavy thinking.

Two days later Jim telephoned Sig. Jim said, "Do you know how sick your man in Minot is?" Sig knew he was bad. "How bad Clutch?" "He is only several weeks, at the most, away from death." Sig's response was. "I'll have to find a replacement." Jim said, "Can I ask you to hold off until I return to Janesville, as a favor to me. I'll talk to you about it as soon as I return next week." Sig answered, "Clutch, I have no trouble doing a favor for you. How are you doing with your sadness? I hope better." "It's difficult Sig, but I am improving". That was the end of the conversation. Jim drove back to Minot one afternoon to visit further with the proprietor of the larger bowling alley. Jim asked how the owner would like to hire him as a manager. He spoke truthfully of his past and present, ownership of auto maintenance shops and bootlegging. He also said he would still be working for the Bellagio Syndicate after moving to Minot but promised that none of that business would be conducted out of the bowling alley. In fact Jim would not be doing any of the bootlegging himself, but would just be an overseer and trouble- shooter. The bowling alley proprietor seemed interested. The bootlegging thing did not scare him off. It was too commonplace. The bowling alley owner said it appeared to him that prohibition was going to be repealed anyway. He said he would be the first business to buy a beer license. He recognized Jim's talents as a manager. Jim promised the owner he would be getting back in several weeks. Jim discussed his plans with Lee and Ann. They highly liked to idea of Jim moving back to North Dakota.

Jim spent the rest of his days at the farm helping Lee with farm work and Ann with hanging new cupboards in Ann's kitchen. Jim took off one day, going to town, with Priscella as help, to buy Christmas presents for everyone. Christmas was fun. Jim had bought a huge turkey from one of the neighbors who had raised a few extra birds. Jim drove all the way to Valley City one day to buy a spruce tree. After dragging it into the living room it had to be shortened a foot. Jim brought boxes of ornaments, including a glass angel for the very top. The tree was illuminated with small candles placed in holders that clamped to the ends of branches. They were lit after Christmas Eve lutefisk supper, several buckets of water standing by in case of an inadvertent fire. Everyone participated in snuffing out the candles before they burned too low. Gifts were opened after the candles were out. Jim had outdone himself with generosity, everyone receiving numerous gifts from him. The turkey dinner on Christmas day put everyone to napping except the dishwashers. They had to stay on their feet. Jim left for Janesville the day after New Years. His departure was joyous because it was quite sure he would soon be returning to live in Minot.

When Clutch arrived in Janesville the next day he drove directly to Lake Geneva to visit with Sig. They had a late night meeting. Clutch outlining his plan to Sig, his desire to move to Minot, North Dakota and manage that area of the Bellagio Syndicate. Clutch told Sig he likely would also be managing a bowling alley but would keep the two businesses entirely separate. Sig said he had called up his man in Minot the night before and he could not even come to the phone, his wife telling Sig that her husband was totally bedridden and was not expected to live more than a couple of days. Sig finished the evening by saying, "Clutch, I give your plan my blessing. We will miss you here in Wisconsin but be comforted to still have you in the business."

Clutch did not have a lot to do to make his move. His apartment had been rented furnished so he had none of that to move. He had closets full of clothes, more than he could get into his Desoto. He had it all packed by a professional packer and placed in storage till he had found a living place in Minot. He sold his Chris Craft boat at a bargain price to a friend living on Lake Geneva. Most of his assets were in cash, hard, cold thousand dollar bills, a good share of it kept in Sig's safe, located in a vault two stories under ground on Sig's Lake Geneva property. Sig told Clutch he could leave it there till he needed it. The cache also contained a few large diamonds, a very wise investment, considering the stock market crash and the precarious condition of banks. Clutch did not liquidate any of his land investments. They were worth very little in cash, but it was his estimate that land values would eventually return. In little more than a week, Clutch was on his way back to North Dakota. His most difficult "Goodbye" was to Sig, the best friend he had ever known.

Clutch stopped in Valley City on the way through North Dakota. He felt emotionally able to visit Joe and Trudy and also say "Hello" to Sparky. Joe and Trudy were delighted to see Clutch but grief stricken when he told them of Sally Jo's death. They were more than surprised when Clutch announced he was moving to Minot. He divulged all his plans to them. Clutch made a very brief stop at Sparky's the next morning. Sparky admitted the depression was cutting into his business. He had let one man go already. He hated to put a man out of work but had to protect the bottom line. Clutch did not tell Sparky about Sally Jo. To repeat the story twice in one day would have been too much.

CHAPTER FIFTEEN

Within two weeks Jim had found a nice apartment in Minot, two bedrooms, large kitchen, dinette, living room, full bath, garage, large storage room in the basement. He was very pleased with it. It was unfurnished. Priscella spent several days with Jim helping him buy furniture and linens. He had his clothes shipped from Janesville by train and before long was right at home. His job of managing the bowling alley worked out well. It kept him occupied. The owner was pleased with the way Jim took over. He and his wife took off on a month trip to California. Jim's job with the syndicate proved unbothersome. He had to twist the arm of a dance hall owner who was behind in his payments. It came to Jim stopping delivery of liquor before the owner paid up. Then, and only then, did Jim restart delivery. There was no problem with bootlegging from Canada by outlaws. The problem had never recurred after Jim rubber out the mischief several years previously.

Jim had been in Minot for two months when his employee in Williston told him, that the sheriff was being difficult. He had closed up a dance hall in Tioga and was threatening the proprietor of a pool hall in Epping to close him down. Jim visited the sheriff at his office in the county jail in Williston. Clutch asked him outright what the problem was, why all of a sudden this tough policy? Wasn't the syndicate paying him enough? It turned out the sheriff did not know that Jim had located in Minot when his predecessor had died. It appeared to Jim that the sheriff wanted his cake and eat it too. Jim advised the sheriff to get back on the track. Jim left the sheriff's office that day not really trusting the man. Jim decided the sheriff lacked "smarts". He may need a little discipline. He talked to Sig on the telephone that night. Sig said, "If that sheriff makes one more bad move haul him to the Missouri River, brake a hole in the ice and give him one cold bath. If he drowns in the process, that will be all right too.

It wasn't one month later when again the sheriff jumped on the pool hall operator in Epping, the sheriff himself drunk, just throwing his weight around. One week later, the sheriff drunk again, pulled into his driveway at his home late at night, and as soon as he stepped out of his car, he was hit hard on the head from behind with a hand maul by a man masked in a black stocking with eye holes in it. A second man stood by, also masked. The second man ran down the street to where a car was parked and signaled the driver to come forward. The limp body of the sheriff was thrown into the trunk, the three masked men driving off down the street, all done quietly in the dark of the night. The car drove south of town to a gravel pit on the banks of the Missouri River. A goodly amount of water flooded the pit, a thick layer of ice on top. The sheriff's body was rolled out of the car trunk, still limped then skidded onto the ice. One of the masked men chopped a hole in the ice. The sheriff's body was pushed into the hole. The cold shock awakened him. The water was not deep. The sheriff stoop up with great trouble and crawled out of the water, staggering both from his drunkenness and the blow on the head. By this time the masked men, in their car, were well away from the gravel pit and racing down the road. The sheriff had a struggle getting to the highway, where, about one half hour later, he was able to stop a car that took him home. Two days later he was in the hospital with pneumonia. His recovery was slow requiring a two-month absence from his office. The truth of his late night predicament never came out, though there were many rumors. He never bothered the pool hall operator again and reduced his own consumption of alcohol for ever after.

1932 V-16 CADILLAC PHAETON

Jim's next assignment was to develop a new route for smuggling Canadian Whiskey into the United States. The United States Custom Stations had closed everything up tight. Driving across the border through wilderness and farm fields was too hazardous and destructive to vehicles. By asking questions and doing some reconnaissance on his own he discovered a crossing at the United States/Canada border where there was no US Customs Post. There was a Canadian Customs Post on the Canadian side of the border but they should not be too difficult to deal with. The Canadians were concerned principally with crossing of people and goods from the US to Canada. The crossing was twenty-five miles north of Mohall on Highway 28. The small village of Sherwood lay on the west side of Highway 28 two miles south of the border. It was a quiet place, pretty much closed down after 6:00PM every evening. It could serve as rendezvous location. Jim stopped one day to visit the customs officer at the Canadian post. Jim talked turkey to him. "Would the officer be interested in a little extra income, allow a Canadian from Regina, Saskatchewan to drive across the border to Sherwood, North Dakota, once a week, on Thursday, about 8:00PM, returning to Canada within an hour. The driver would pay the Customs officer on duty $50 cash each trip. The officer Jim was talking to said, "I will try to arrange my schedule to be on duty myself at that time, or be here myself anyway to avoid any hitches." Next Jim drove to Sherwood, looking for a building he could rent to serve as a transfer spot. He found an old abandoned blacksmith shop a block off main street, just the right size for two automobiles to drive inside out of public view. The son of the old smithy lived in town. Jim ran him down at the local pool hall and rented the old building for $25 a year. The doors had a hasp on them. Jim bought a padlock at the local hardware store, locked up the old building and drove to Regina that afternoon, looked up his supplier that evening, sealing the end of the deal.

Jim telephone Sig the next day describing the arrangements he had made to smuggle in Canadian Whiskey. Sig was pleased. Jim said, "If we need it, I believe the volume obtainable via this new route is unlimited." Sig insisted Jim visit them late summer for some days at the lake and a weekend in Chicago. Jim accepted.

CHAPTER SIXTEEN

The bowling alley was closed on Sundays, Jim's day off. He fell into the habit of driving down to the farm early every Sunday morning. It was comforting to be with the family. Ann's Sunday dinners were always a treat. The family would usually not be home from church when Jim arrived. He would make himself at home, maybe filling his pockets with apples from the barrel in the cellar, and then heading for the barn to pass them out to the horses. Queen would recognize Jim's footsteps before he would open the barn door, and give a loud whinny as a greeting. The other horses would join in to compose a six-part chorus. Jim would tease them a bit, not entering the barn immediately. That stimulated them to whinny all the louder. Jim was always careful to portion out the apples equally. Lee's mare, Babe had a new spring colt. What a sharpie, shy but loveable. There were twelve newborn spring calves in a pen by the front door. They were being fed a diet of skim milk with some ground barley mixed in. One bull calf was segregated in a small pen, being fed nothing but skim milk, grooming him to be butchered in three months for veal. The meat would be white as breast of chicken from his receiving no iron in his diet. In was now the very last of March. The cows would soon be put out to pasture. After several days the cream would come out of the separator a bright colored yellow, picking up the hue from the fresh green grass indulged by the cows. Lee had to be careful not to allow the cattle to over eat their spring diet, putting them to pasture only every other day at the start. They might develop 'bloat'.

Lee had a flock of fifty sheep. The ewes had all lambed, the last one just the day before one of Jim's Sunday visits, twins, no less, the fourth pair this spring. The day old pair were still in the sheep shed with their mother, the rest in the pasture. Jim looked in on the newborns. They were doing fine, though mother was having some difficulty satisfying their appetites. Jim noticed a half full nursing bottle of milk on the shelf. He warmed it in his armpit for a while, and then gave the two lambs turns on the nipple. They had the bottle empty in no time. Mother did not seem to mind Jim's attending her babies. Next Jim would check on the chicken coop. The hens were into their heavy spring production time. Jim would gather some eggs in a pail. Ann had not received delivery of her chicks from the hatchery yet. That would be soon. They would go in a separate room in the chicken house under a heated brooder. She had ordered two hundred leghorns. Jim completed his visits to his farm friends by checking on five nesting Peking hen ducks in a hay filled section of the chicken house that had a small exit door to allow the ducks access to the various puddles scatted around the farm yard. Jim did not visit the hog barn, that not being his favorite location. The sows had not pigged their piglets anyway. That would not be until May. They then would each choose their own farrowing hut out of the dozen scattered around the hog pasture. Jim would usually have his visits to the farm creatures completed by the time the family arrived home from church. Ann would rush into the house to bring dinner to completion. Pot roast was on the menu. Ann had pre-boiled the potatoes and carrots on Saturday. Both vegetables had been carried over in the cellar from the previous years garden, the potatoes piled on the floor in the corner, the carrots buried in a box full of sand. Fresh bread and apple pie had been baked early Sunday morning. Ice cream had been whipped up and placed in the freezing compartment of the kerosene refrigerator on Saturday. Lee had bought a battery-operated radio the previous summer. He and Jim moved up close to the speaker to listen to the activist Catholic priest, Father Coughlin, give his weekly speech from Detroit. He was arousing strong antagonism against the politicians in Washington, D.C. His spiel was entertaining. Soon Ann called the family to the table. She received many compliments on the dinner. Everyone begged for small portions of the apple pie alamode, saying they would eat more of it later. The afternoon passed quickly with long chair naps by the men. When Jim left that evening he invited Lee and Ann to drive to Minot some afternoon for several lines of bowling. Lee had bowled some, Ann hadn't. They took Jim up on his invitation the next Wednesday and had a great time, so much so they returned every Wednesday until spring field and garden work kept them on the farm.

Jim's work for the syndicate went well all summer. He developed good rapport with the county sheriffs in northwest North Dakota and northeast Montana. All of the sheriff's wives received silver fox neckpieces that fall. He had hired a man to make the runs to Sherwood, now three a week. The same man also delivered booze to Williston, Mandan, Jamestown and Devil's Lake in North Dakota as well as three cities in South Dakota. The syndicate man in Williston served eastern Montana. Jim had plenty to keep him busy. The booze shipped in from the east, mainly out of Milwaukee, came by train, disguised as various types of freight, table dishes one time, clocks another, mirrors another, always packed with excelsior in wooden boxes, in other shapes than whiskey cases. Any unpacking or re-packing was done in an old barn on the edge of town, then carried right out from there to the other cities. Nothing was ever left in storage.

CHAPTER SEVENTEEN

Jim took a week off late summer to drive to Wisconsin to visit Sig and his family. They entertained him royally, taking him to Chicago for several days. The Italian Opera Company was in town. Sig loved opera. They saw "Figeratto". Sig said the beautiful music played in his ears for days. Jim found his friend enjoying the Chris Craft Jim had sold him. Jim drove up to Milwaukee on the way back home, visiting Sally Jo's grave and spending the evening with her parents. There were tears shed by all when Jim left.

Jim, Lee and Sven spent several weekends hunting pheasants that fall. Jim had bought a two-year-old English Pointer, Princess, that summer, fully trained for upland game. She was beauty, could hold a point indefinitely, never flushing birds ahead of the hunters. Jim paid a high price for her, but she was worth it. Jim fell into the habit of driving out into the country south of Minot nearly every morning that fall during pheasant season. The bowling alley didn't open till noon. It was a bad morning when he and Princess wouldn't come back to town with a couple of roosters. Plenty of his friends were glad to take them off Jim's hands. Jim and Princess became inseparable, Princess staying with him at the bowling alley till it closed, every day, sleeping by his bedside every night and going into the cafes with him when he ate out.

Jim and his duck-hunting friend of several years past, Vince O'Leary, made two trips to Lake Peterson late that fall for some great duck hunting. They took three days for one of the trips, staying in a Green Gable cabin in the City of Turtle Lake. It was the most enjoyable time Jim had since Sally Jo's death, taking the tragedy off his mind as he and Vince fired their guns, as birds flew past, pumping their wings fast in a northwest wind with snowflakes flying horizontal the last day of the hunt. Vince and Jim cleaned their birds each evening. They had a bushel basket full to haul home. Jim gave most of his share to friends in Minot.

Thanksgiving dinner was at Peterson's this fall of 1931. Sven and Priscella were still living with Sven's folks. It was a crowded household with Sven's five siblings and Priscella and Sven's two children, but they had learned to stay out of each other's hair. There had been plans for building another house on the farm site so that Sven, Priscella and their children could have their own place. The depression was changing those plans. The weather turned bad on Thanksgiving Day. A Class "A" Prairie Blizzard started blowing out of the northwest in the forenoon while the Doyers were driving over to the Petersons. They were heading south with the wind mainly behind them. Heavy snow was accumulating on the road. Jim's Desoto was not too good in snow, to low slung. They made it to the Peterson's, but as they turned there into their lane, heading west, the visibility turned to zero, a total white out. Jim had trouble staying on the lane. Lee had to get out and walk in front of the car for a ways until they came into the lea of the buildings and grove. When they arrived, Sven was in the barn harnessing up a team of horses planning to head out, thinking Jim may have driven off the road and would need a pull. Sven was relieved to see the Desoto drive into the yard. Sven had Jim run his car into the machine shed after unloading his passengers at the back door. The Peterson's kitchen was glowing with warmth. It felt comfy to the Doyer's, especially to Lee after his walk in front of the car. Jim took a bottle of brandy out of his inside overcoat pocket and passed it around the kitchen. Everyone put it to their lips and tipped their heads back, even those who had not been out in the blizzard.

The day had started out balmy with rain falling. When the rain turned to snow, about the time the Doyer's left their place, the thermometer dropped precipitously. It was already down to zero. Obviously the two families were isolated for the day, maybe longer. This type of storm tended to last several days. Lee was now wishing he had stayed home, in fear of not getting home to attend to his livestock. There could be some miserable milk cows that evening. The best that could happen would be for the calves to break out of their pen and nurse the cows, relieving them of the congestion in their udders. This concern was spoiling Lee's day. Vince kept reassuring Lee that he would get home. His one team of horses could travel through anything, never get lost, and never get off the road. The Peterson ladies had cooked masterfully for this big day. The main course of the dinner not only included a turkey with chestnut dressing, but also molasses/peach glazed ham, mashed potatoes, sweet potatoes, acorn squash slices baked in butter and angel food cake with strawberry preserves and whipped topping for dessert.

Everyone took a nap after the dishes were washed and dried, some on the floor, some on cushioned chairs in the living room, some in the bedrooms, everyone except Lee. He paced the floor, going outside frequently to check on the storm, which he wasn't finding any better. About 3:00PM he woke up Sven and said "I am going to take you up on your offer to bring me home with the horses and sleigh. The two men dressed as warm as possible, wool underwear, wool shirts and pants, wool socks, wool gloves, everything possible wool. They had on fur caps and fur mitts that reached halfway up their forearms, flannel lined coveralls, fur-out buffalo coats with high collars reaching over the tops of their heads and fur lined boots. They could barely get out the door. They cleaned the snow out of the four-runner dray sleigh and filled it with hay. In the barn they threw winter blankets over the horses to the sleigh. It was 3:30PM when they pulled out of the yard. Those watching from in the house lost sight of them when they were less than fifty yards down the lane. The blowing snow completely enveloped them. The two men could not tell when they reached the corner of the lane with the road. The horses sensed it perfectly, making an exact turn at the corner and heading straight north into the wind. It amazed Lee and Sven how the horses stayed on the road, not straying into the ditches. It was three miles straight to the Doyer's place. The horses walked a slow, steady gait. The wind was ferocious. Lee and Vince lay down in the hay, not able to see ahead. That was trusted to the horses. It took nearly an hour to cover the three miles. Lee sat up when he thought they were near his lane. All of a sudden the horses hesitated. Vince gave a gentle tug on the reins to the left. The horses responded. They headed down the lane. Five minutes and they were in the yard. Vince put the horses in the barn. Lee went to the house to stoke the fires. He called the Petersons. The ring got through. Priscella answered. Her voice could barely be heard. Lee screamed, "We are at the Doyers!" She got the message, much relieved. It took two hours for Lee and Sven to do chores. Hauling up the slop to the hog house was the worst but the hogs appreciated the effort. It had turned dark and the wind had not decreased in velocity. There was so much snow blowing it was difficult to tell if any of it was still falling from the sky. Sven made no hint of trying to head back home in the dark. He telephoned Priscella and screamed, "I am staying here". The two men fixed themselves a supper of leftovers they pulled out of the refrigerator. They were dead tired from the ordeal of the storm. Lee banked the fires and the two men were in bed by 9:30.

Sven helped Lee with the chores again in the morning. After a breakfast of two pork chops, dug out of the lard crock in the cellar and fried eggs and potatoes. Sven decided the storm had abated sufficiently for him to head home. Sven reported some big drifts to Jim when he arrived, too big for the Desoto. That meant another night at the Petersons. The turkey had been cleaned down to the bones and the ham was becoming smaller by the hour. Mid-morning the next day they saw the snow plow drive down the road, a cloud of snow three stories high flying off to its side. Jim and his passengers left shortly after. The snowplow had cleared the road of drifts. By the time they reached Doyer's lane, Lee had been out with his big, rock weighted wooden V-plow to clear the lane and the yard paths. Jim headed back to Minot right after lunch.

Jim talked to the owner of the bowling alley that winter about some improvements; a name change with a neon sign out front. Jim suggested the name be changed from Roy's Alleys to THE FAST LANES—**Bowling, Pool-Billiards, Restaurant, Ice Cream Bar**, improvement in the restaurant menu, construction of an addition for a sit down dining room, and an ice cream bar with a drive up window for the summer trade, with car service by a blow of the horn, with two carhops ready to respond. Jim had already talked the local ice cream manufacturer into increasing the number of flavors, including peach, strawberry, mixed nut, coffee and last but not least spumoni. Jim had been introduced to that by Sig. The rainbow of colors could vary, but the most common was red, green and orange. Jim had seen these innovations in Chicago, Milwaukee and other Wisconsin cities. Roy though Jim was ahead of his time and was concerned about investing more money, what with the severe depression. Jim said he would put up the money if Roy would make him a partner. This was the first indication to Roy that Jim had money. Jim talked Roy into it. They had an attorney write a partnership. Jim made a quick trip to Lake Geneva for some cash out of Sig's vault. When Jim told Sig of his plans, it sounded good. He said, "I think I may start an ice cream parlor and drive up ice cream bar at Lake Geneva. I may seek a Bridgeman's franchise. I have seen them in Chicago. It's time for me to diversify. The future for the bootlegging business is not rosy. Repeal of Prohibition is around the corner" Jim stopped in Janesville before returning to Minot. He wanted to look at the new 1932 model of the V-16 CADILLAC PHAETON. It was considered the favorite car of bootleggers, advertised as having the *Power of an Airplane under the Hood of the Car*. The model on the showroom floor was a tourist style, four door, roll back on top, two spare tires mounted on the back ends of both front fenders, on a chrome cover. Trumpet horns stuck out a foot on each side of the chrome radiator grill. Two road lights, a necessity of bootleggers, were mounted on the front bumper, also chrome. Everything was chrome. The rear trunk could hold eight cases of liquor. The car salesman made a point of this feature. He knew Jim and what he did for a living. The wheels were beautifully spoked and chromed, the tires white walled. The body was painted tan, the fenders and running boards a deep port wine color. It was rated as the king of the road. Jim struck a good deal with the car salesman, receiving a high trade in value for his Desoto. Because of the depression, it was a buyer's market. It had only ten miles on it. Jim had to drive it slow all the way to Minot to break in the engine. The trip took him three days. The car drew a big group of admirers wherever it was parked. Roy thought it would draw customers to the FAST LANE.

Christmas 1931 and New Years 1932 came and went. Sven asked Jim, kiddingly, if he wouldn't wasn't to keep the Cadillac Phaeton in his machine shed. Jim declined. Princess never strayed out of the front passenger seat and accepted it being covered with a blanket. The improvements on the FAST LANES were started mid winter with a promise to be completed by May 1st. The sign was installed in April. It hung out over the corner of the building, lighting up the area in all directions. A smaller sign over the drive up window invited customers to blow their horns for service. A private Grand Opening Party was held on May Day, a complimentary dinner for City and County office holders and local businessmen. Free pool-billiards and bowling were offered before and after dinner. The meat was beef au juice, thick sliced from prime roasts. The dessert was spumoni ice cream and orange/mint bars. The guests were impressed. Roy's comment was, "Jim, you know how to throw a party". The next day was open house for the public, half price for everything; bowling, pool-billiards, food and ice cream. The place was jammed from opening to closing. On several occasions that spring Jim had noticed a cute young blonde at the FAST LANES, bowling with a group of schoolteachers, all girls. More leagues and teams were forming by the end of the week. He asked a friend about her. Her name was Edna Jagersson. She taught English at the junior high school. She was from a small town west of Minot where she had graduated from high school and than taken an additional year in the normal training department to qualify as a country schoolteacher. She obtained a job that next year at a rural school, living with one of the school board member's families. The school board member took her to school every morning and picked her up every late afternoon. Her life was very isolated, far from the main stream. She had twelve students from first to sixth grade, two of them to graduate in the spring. The graduation exercise the end of May included all of the sixth grade graduates from throughout the county, held in the high school auditorium in Minot. It was a gala affair with County Commissioners and all of the teachers from every rural school sitting on the stage. The town band provided music, to include several solos by locals. The County Superintendent handed out the diplomas. Edna had a very disturbing thing happen to her that spring. One evening on the way home with Mr. Torkelsson he grabbed Edna, pulling him towards her forcefully and kissing her right on the lips. She pushed him away and jumped out her side of the buggy, running to a nearby farmhouse. Mr. Torkelsson whipped the horses to chase after her. Edna reached the house before he did. The farm wife was in the yard working in her garden. Edna ran to her. Between breaths she told the farm lady what happened. Torkelsson was getting out of his buggy. The farm lady picked up her hoe, raising it over her head and told Torkelsson to get off her property, quick as he could. He hesitated. The farm lady advanced towards him, raising the hoe higher. Torkelsson backed towards the buggy and climbed in. The horse was as scared as Torkelsson was. He turned around, nearly tipping the buggy and took off back down the lane, dust flying, and the farm lady screaming at Torkelsson to leave Edna alone or he would be a dead man. The farm lady told Edna, "I never did trust Torkelsson". She went right into the house, called the chairman of the board, who wasn't home, but told the whole thing to his wife. Torkelsson was never heard from again. Another board member took Edna back and forth to school the rest of the year. Edna went to summer school at the University of North Dakota in Grand Forks in June, earning enough credits to obtain her high school teaching certificate, thus getting her job in the Minot school. She loved her placement and had been rehired for the coming year. She roomed in a private home near the high school in Minot. Jim and Edna saw a lot of each other at the FAST LANES. Jim never built up the courage to ask her for a date. The closest he got to that was to give Edna a ride home one evening in his Cadillac Phaeton. He did escort her to the door of her house, only saying 'goodbye'. Before he knew it she was off to Grand Forks. Jim had his eye on no one else. He tended to his two businesses full time.

Neither Jim nor Edna wrote each other all summer. Who can say if each even thought of the other? Everyone's mind was on the up coming National election in November. Democratic Party Presidential Candidate Franklin Delano Roosevelt and his running mate, Vice-presidential Candidate John Vance Garner, crisscrossed the United States by train many times during their campaign. Their train passed through Minot one early morning in August with an announced time arrival of 7:00AM. The train tracks were lined with crowds of people for a mile both east and west of the depot, just to get a look at Roosevelt to shout, "I love North Dakota". The crowd shouted, "We love you". They were enamored. He campaigned for repeal of Prohibition. That did not bother Jim.

Edna returned to Minot in late August. A friend of Jim's had told Jim she was back from college. Several days later Jim spotted Edna sitting with some other teachers at the FAST LANES indoor ice cream bar. He sat down beside the group. They all moved over so there would be an empty seat beside Edna. Jim said, "It's nice to see you back". Edna said, "It's nice to be back". Jim responded with, "I hope we can see more of each other this year. How about going to a movie with me tonight?" "I would love to", she said. "I'll pick you up at 8:30, ok." "Ok" Edna responded. They drove down to the FAST LANES after the movie, joining a group of young couples that had been bowling and were now eating lunch. Jim and Edna stayed till it was time for Jim to lock the place up. They drove around town for a while before they stopped in front of Edna's rooming house. Jim snuggled over to Edna. She put her head on his shoulder. There was one small kiss at the front door but Jim knew he would be back. Edna knew Jim would be back.

Jim and Edna dated frequently. Jim knew Edna was not an easy make. He made no attempt to interest her in sexual intercourse. Their relationship reached high temperatures at times but he received signals, which informed him that he had better back off. Edna attended the First Norwegian Church every Sunday. Jim attended with her only occasionally, other Sundays excusing himself to attend to business matters. In the election that fall, North Dakota and the nation voted strongly for the democrats and Roosevelt.

Jim invited Edna to spend Thanksgiving Day with his family. The Doyers put on their best for Jim's girlfriend. They impressed her and she impressed them. The promise was for Jim to spend Christmas with Edna's family. That also worked out well. Jim had a big party at the FAST LANES on New Years Eve, decorations, noisemakers, crepe paper hats, midnight lunch, the whole package at a special price. The place was jammed. The couple went to Jim's apartment after the celebration. Jim proposed, bringing out a diamond as big as a chicken's eyeball. Edna swooned. She accepted his proposal. They kissed passionately. Both were extremely happy, on clouds. No wedding plans were made that night. Edna stayed all night at Jim's apartment. They did not go to bed together. Edna slept on the sofa. They fixed a big breakfast on New Years Day morning, celebrating their engagement. They each telephoned their families that day to announce their commitment. Everyone was thrilled.

In February of that year of 1933 the United States Congress voted to submit to the states the 21st Amendment (Repeal of Prohibition). In March, Congress passed the 3.2 beer law. By May there were thirty states selling beer, including North Dakota. Hard liquor soon followed. Jim decided to get out of the bootlegging business promptly. There wasn't going to be any bootlegging anyway. Jim telephoned his decision to Sig, who understood. The voters of Minot decided to issue a limited number of beer licenses. THE FAST LANES applied and acquired one. Jim had never told Edna the whole story of his bootlegging and Edna never asked a lot of questions. The two of them made a quick decision in May to have a June wedding. Edna's family, particularly her mother, was in a tizzy about such short notice. There was no talking Jim or Edna into a later date. They were both deeply in love and wanted to fulfill their love with marriage. The date was set for Saturday, June 25th at 3:00PM, the place, at Edna's family church in the town of Stanley, west of Minot. One of Edna's schoolteacher friends was the maid of honor; another friend and her two younger sisters were bridesmaids. Joe came up from Valley City to be Jim's best man. Jim's brothers, Shane and Winston, and a friend from Minot made up the rest of the groom's attendants. The weather on the wedding day was perfect, the kind made for weddings. The reception was in the church basement, tables set for seventy-five guests. Flowers were everywhere. A group of the younger men stole the bride, late in the afternoon, but did not keep her for long. When Jim and Edna took off in the Cadillac Phaeton, half of the tin cans in Stanley were tied to the rear bumper. They drove up and down the streets with a long procession of autos behind them, all blowing their horns.

Finally Jim left town on US Hwy 2, heading west. He pressed the accelerator of the Phaeton to the floor, leaving the followers behind in quick order. Jim had reserved the bridal suite in the Sherman Hotel in Williston. They stopped first at the home of an uncle and aunt of Edna's, five miles west of Stanley to change clothes and get rid of what cans were left tied to the rear bumper. They did not waste any time at all. After checking into their room at the Sherman Hotel and cleaning up a little bit in their suite, they went back down to the main floor dining room. Jim knew the hotel had a lounge to serve liquor. He asked the matre de if he would show it to them. He did through a locked door at the back of the dining room, hidden by several artificial palm trees. Hard liquor had not yet been permitted in North Dakota, but they had no trouble getting a bottle of champagne to celebrate their wedding night. They ate light, chicken ala king on toast. They were in their suite by 9:00 PM, both eager to consummate the marriage. Edna put on a lovely new silk nightgown she had purchased for the occasion. She looked fetching as she exited the dressing room. Jim was sitting on the chaise waiting for her, he attired in a silk robe imported from Japan. He stood up, pulled Edna into his arms, hugging her tight, kissing her hard on the lips first, then on the neck then on the bosom, before returning to Edna's lips. She was so warm and supple, nearly molten. Jim sat down on the chaise, bringing Edna down beside him, embracing her again, and kissing her over and over. They had not spoken till Edna said, "Jim, I am so happy. I love you so much. You are so important to me." Jim answered, "Edna, I have never been so thrilled and content with my life. You mean everything to me." Without any more conversation, Jim stood up, taking Edna's hand to stand her up. He put his hand around her waist and walked her into the bedroom. Waiting till the marriage night for coition had been a good choice.

Jim had made reservations on the Great Northern Empire Builder to travel to Glacier Park, Montana. They left the Cad in the hotel garage and took a taxi to the station. The train was on time with departure at 10:30AM. They had no more than settled into their first class compartment and then it was time for lunch. They each ordered cold turkey sandwiches. Jim had fresh strawberry pie for dessert, Edna orange sherbet. They finished off with coffee. Back in the compartment, they both dozed in their chairs. After her nap, Edna read a Sinclair Lewis book she had brought along. Jim read a Zane Gray novel he had bought at the news stand in the Williston station. The stops at the stations were brief. Soon Wolf Point, Glasgow and Malta were behind them. The stop at Havre was 10 minutes. Both Jim and Edna got off the train and walked up and down the platform to stretch their legs. They smooched a lot in their compartment, fortifying their love. Their destination that evening was East Glacier Hotel. The train arrived at the station at 6:55PM. A Native American Indian Chief in full regal headdress met the tourists on the station platform. A bus painted bright red took the hotel guests from the station to the hotel, only a half mile away. All the buildings were of Swiss mountain architecture, this prevailing for all the hotels in Glacier Park.

CHAPTER EIGHTEEN

Jim and Edna's first night in the hotel was quiet and cozy. They both had baked Pacific salmon with creamed fresh asparagus spikes for dinner. They finished off their meal with crème de menthe on vanilla ice cream and Armenian coffee. They were early to bed, hungry for the amour of the honeymoon. Their room was on the second story of the hotel on the north side, towards the mountains, which presented a beautiful view when they awoke in the morning. They ate breakfast in the dining room, departing the hotel at 10:00AM, on one of the bright red busses, for Two Medicine Chalet, in an isolated location on the shore of a small glacier fed Lake at the head of a mountain peaked canyon. The path to the chalet entrance crossed the rushing waters of the outlet creek, over an arched bridge. Jim stopped at the top of the bridge looking in the water to see it was full of cutthroat trout. He said, "Edna, we are going to find a couple of fly rods and have us some fish." She said, "Do not be so sure, maybe they are somebody's pets." A bellhop carried their luggage to their room on the second floor. He opened the room's windows to a view across the lake, and a gentle breeze of cool air, snow capped mountains as a backdrop. Lunch was being served in the dining room so they went back downstairs. The chalet accommodated only sixteen guests so the crowd was small. Jim and Edna's reservation was for one week. Clam Chowder and BLT sandwich was the lunch. After lunch Jim asked at the front desk about fishing. He was told fly rods could be rented at the boathouse. The boat boy sold spinners, worms and dry flies. Creels, landing nets and rowboats were also for rent and the boat boy would have some suggestions as to where to catch the most fish. Jim was also promised that the fish would be served to him in the dining room if he met with success. Jim talked to the boat boy that afternoon to make arrangements for fishing the next morning, early, too early for Edna. That afternoon they strolled a path around the lake. It was so pleasant. The outing gave them an appetite for dinner. The menu was restricted, given the small number of guests. The choice was a T-bone steak or broiled St. Mary Lake whitefish. Jim took the steak, Edna the fish. They were seated that evening at a table for four with another young couple, also on their honeymoon, they being from Portland, Oregon. They told of having taken the train to West Glacier Station, bus from there to Lake McDonald Hotel for one night, then horseback on a beautiful trail to Sperry Glacier Chalet where they spent two nights and a day trip onto Sperry Glacier before descending to Going To The Sun Chalet for a night. From there they had taken a boat to St. Mary Chalet, where they took a bus again, ending up in Many Glacier Hotel for a night. Then on to Two Medicine Chalet, where they were going to spend two nights before riding the bus to East Glacier Hotel for a night and then back to Portland again by train. What a trip. Maybe that would be next year for Jim and Edna.

Jim rose very early the next morning, before sunrise. He moved around the room quietly to avoid disturbing Edna, but she heard him anyway and asked for a kiss before he left the room. The boat boy had rented him a small backpack for his gear and the kitchen had prepared him a husky trail lunch and a thermos of coffee. His plan was to hike to the upper end of the lake, fish the shallows and a distance up the inlet creek, all the way to the upper lake, if necessary to catch his limit of trout. It was slow going on the trail when he first started out in the dark of night and he being poorly dark-adapted. He sang and whistled to himself, to make sure any grizzly bears or black bears would hear him coming, although they hadn't been a problem around Two Medicine, there being no campground with garbage cans to attract them. The sky was brightening in the east by the time he was three-fourths his way to the end of the lake. He stopped to rest and have a cup of coffee. Before getting back on the trail he donned his waders, tied a Royal Coachmen dry fly on the end of his leader, walked away from shore and cast out. On his third cast he had a fish hit the fly. Jim let the fish have it for a few seconds then set the hook. He had him, a snappy little fighter. Jim unsnapped his landing net, wound in the fish, then netted him to pride himself in having a ten-inch cutthroat, in the creel with some wet grass. He received no more activity in that spot so he moved on to the end of the lake. There he found a deep pool where the creek tumbled into the lake. Three more trout, all cutthroats, took his Royal Coachman. Two were too small to keep. The other one went in his creel. He waded up stream till he came to another deep pool. A twelve inch cut throat lay under a rock waiting for a morsel to drift by. He hit Jim's fly, breaking water with a splash. He was big enough to give Jim a five-minute play, then into the creel. Jim's luck waned. The Royal Coachmen lost its allure. Jim tied a Mepps spinner on his leader, carefully threading a small angleworm on the treble hook. That did the trick. He soon had the three more fish to fill his limit, more than enough for a meal for Edna and himself. After hiking back down to the lake he opened up his bag lunch; two chicken drumsticks, a buttered roll, three raw carrots and a box of raisins. His coffee had turned cool, but it quenched his thirst. He lay in the sun on a huge lakeshore rock and dozed off to sleep for a short nap before starting back to the chalet. Edna was sitting on the front balcony waiting for him when she spotted him coming down the trail. She ran off the balcony to meet him, throwing her arms around him, saying, "I missed you so much all day, Honey!" Jim said, "Same for me Edna." Then he opened his creel to show his fish, saying, "The kitchen is going to fix these for our dinner." After returning his gear to the boathouse, he went into their room for a shower and clean clothes. Edna followed him. Before Jim dressed they had a good smooching session on the bed. It was nearing dinnertime. Edna freshened herself up before the two went down to the lobby. There was a small bar room off the lobby where you could fix your own drink. The guests had to furnish their own liquor. The park Authorities had not granted liquor licenses yet. The trout dinner was delicious. They shared the fish with another young couple that were seated at their table, new arrivals at the chalet. The sun had set behind the mountains by the time they had finished eating. The four sat out on the balcony, watching the cloudless western sky turn orange, then red, then pink, and then illuminate the peaks with an alpine glow till the stars twinkled on with the onset of darkness. By then it was turning cold outdoors. The two couples went inside where a burning fireplace was warming the lobby. They played a few hands of hearts before drowsiness overtook them. The electricity at the chalet was produced by a diesel generator, which was turned off at 10:30PM. They decided to retire early to bed.

Jim and Edna spent the rest of their days at Two Medicine Chalet being lazy. They took a few short hikes on the extensive trail system, one day renting horses for a longer trail ride, another day renting a rowboat for a trip up the lake, each time taking trail lunches to enjoy at noon time. The day before their stay was up they took a bus trip to Many Glacier Hotel, stopping at St. Mary's Chalet for lunch. From the road they could see the construction up on the mountain that was taking place to build Going to the Sun Highway over Logan Pass of the Continental Divide. It had been in progress for several years and had several more to go before completion. A similar project was taking place on the other side of The Divide, starting from Lake McDonald. The two projects would meet at the top of the pass when completed, providing the only road through the park, east and west. That afternoon the bus drove north to Watertown Lake Hotel, located in the Canada portion of the Glacier/Watertown International Peace Park. The hotel is located on an elevation of land that provides a spectacular view of the lake with a backdrop of snowcapped mountains. Jim and Edna had but a few minutes to soak in the scenery. Evening coolness was setting in when the bus headed south to Two Medicine. The bus driver had to stop and put the canvas top on. Even at that, the woolen lap robe provided to each passenger, felt good. Most of the chalet guests had been served when Jim and Edna returned to enter the dining room.

CHAPTER NINETEEN

The departure from Two Medicine the next day was late in the afternoon. They did not board the train till evening, in time for dinner at the diner. The bed in their compartment was made up when they returned after eating. They would be arriving in Williston early morning. The compartment was comfy. They slept well. The Pullman attendant brought them juice, toast and coffee to their compartment in the morning, they're being no time to go to the dining room. A taxi ride to the hotel and they were soon off in the Cad to Minot. Edna had given up her place at the rooming house. They were setting up house in Jim's apartment. The complexion of his pad changed significantly with the Edna moving in. Edna enjoyed cooking. She couldn't change Jim's habit of eating lunch at the FAST LANES, but Jim did have breakfast at home and Edna prepared a wholesome dinner each evening. Edna had signed a contract to go back to her teaching job in the fall. Time became heavy on her hands that summer so she started helping Jim at the FAST LANES. The 3.2 beer license had attracted more and more customers. Jim could not handle both the beer bar and serve as a cashier for the restaurant and ice cream bar. Edna came down each forenoon and handled the dining room and cashiers job till after the evening dinner rush. That was the end of evening dinner at home. She enjoyed being a part of it. She wasn't afraid of work. They missed her when she went back to her teaching job that fall, though she did come down most late afternoons to help out over the supper hour, usually going home before Jim, who most often stayed till closing at midnight. Jim bought Edna a Model A Ford Coupe for her own transportation. She looked pretty snappy wheeling around town. Jim's stepsiblings, Kim and Helen, loved to visit Jim and Edna on weekends. Lee and Ann would usually bring the kids into

Minot Friday evening, having dinner in the restaurant themselves. Kim and Helen loved to hang out at the FAST LANES on Saturday and Sunday, Kim keeping the pool/billiard tables in order, Helen bussing dishes. Jim paid them an honest wage, which pleased them. Edna's two sisters visited occasionally, usually to do a little shopping in Minot.

Jim never talked much to Edna about his previous loves, Josephine and Sally Jo. He had told Edna about Sally Jo's tragic death, but not about their cohabitation. Edna had no past affairs; Jim was her first and only serious lover. Jim was now engulfed in the marriage to Edna and his partnership in the FAST LANES. His past mattered very little to him, certainly not deserving of either thought or talk.

Jim took a week off from work in August to go on a fishing trip with three friends. They traveled north into Saskatchewan, Canada, destination; a fishing resort on Big Quill Lake, noted for its Walleyed Pike and Northern Pike. The four were in one cabin. They did none of their own cooking, eating all their meals in the lodge. The fish were abundant. The day's catch was cleaned each evening, preserved in a locker of ice chips. Many were eaten for shore lunch and some prepared for the evening dinner twice during the week. It was a fun, relaxing week but Jim missed Edna. Later the same month Edna spent a few days with her family on the farm. It was enjoyable to be home, but appreciated to be back with Jim. When Edna had to return to her teaching job, she was less than enthusiastic. She wondered if she wouldn't be happier if she would share her time between the FAST LANES and her new husband. Then when she realized in November she was pregnant, she knew she did not want to be teaching full time. She turned in her resignation for as soon as they could find a replacement. The school found a replacement willing to start right after the first of the year.

CHAPTER TWENTY

About the same time, Jim decided he would like to own the FAST LANES by himself, no partner. The partnership agreement Jim and Roy had drawn up contained a buy-sell clause, which meant if Jim offered Roy a price to buy out Roy's half, and Roy did not like the offer, he would have to buy Jim out at the same price. Roy did not like the $25,000 offer Jim gave him. He chose to buy out Jim at the same price. He had a little trouble getting the money together but within the one-month term of the agreement managed to talk his banker into a sufficient loan and the deal was closed. Jim was out, but he had a backup plan. He had been talking to the beer distributors, asking them if they had knowledge of voids in the recreational business in any nearby areas. Several had mentioned the town of Fessenden, the county seat of Wells County. The city was seventy-five miles southeast of Minot on Hwy 52. It had a population of about one thousand and served a large rural area. One other town in Wells County, Harvey, was larger, but not being the county seat, attracted no more business. The beer distributors told Jim that Fessenden was hurting for a good pool hall and bar. Jim and Edna drove to Fessenden one January day to look it over. They were impressed with the quality of the town. It had suffered its bumps from the Great Depression, like all farm communities, but was making a good recovery. There were places of business that had closed during the depression and for all practical purposes were still abandoned. Jim and Edna noticed a large empty building on Main Street that had obviously been an automotive garage and automobile agency, in good condition on the outside, probably built in the late 20's, now empty. Jim inquired at a nearby gas station to find the owner of the property. It was owned by one of the two banks in town, they having repossessed it in 1930 because of default on a mortgage. Jim talked to the loan officer at the bank who informed Jim the property was definitely for sale. The bank was asking only $1000 for the property, it being obvious they wanted to get rid of it. Jim offered the back $900. They accepted his offer. He paid them cash on the spot. Jim knew it was going to take a lot of work to redo the interior into what he wanted. Edna said she would be willing to be a part of the project with the limitations of her pregnancy and raising a child, or maybe more children.

The plans Jim had in mind were for the building to contain their living quarters in the back end of the building. Construction of that portion would be done first. During that period they would need other living quarters. Jim wanted to give up his apartment in Minot as soon as possible. That same day Edna found a room with a kitchenette and bath for rent, furnished. Jim hired a carpenter that same day to start work immediately. Jim would be his helper. Two days later they were loading all their belongings in Minot onto a moving van. They had it all placed in the center of the building in Fessenden and covered with heavy canvas. The first part of the project was to put in a hardwood floor furred up from the existing concrete floor, high enough to hold furnace ducts, water, sewer, and electrical to all parts of the building. The oil burning, forced air furnace located in a small basement, was in good shape but too small to adequately heat the entire building. Jim traded it in on a larger one. The living quarters, with two bedrooms, were ready to occupy in four months, painting and decorating yet to be done.

The next stage of construction was the front part of the building, the bar and pool/billiards area. Jim also had plans for the center of the building, a dry cleaning establishment. There was not a drycleaners in town. Each portion of the building would have a separate entrance to the outdoors but there would also be indoor passageways form one section to the other. Construction went quickly. Edna's due date was July 12th. She delivered in the local hospital on

July 11th, an eight-pound boy, healthy as an ox. Jim was an extraordinary proud father, bragging to everyone. Edna stayed in the hospital 10 days. Her mother came to stay with her at home for two weeks. Mother and child did well. Edna finished up the painting in the apartment she had not finished before the baby was born. The baby was baptized Frank James Doyer when he was three weeks old. Jim and Edna had not affiliated with any church in Fessenden so the ceremony and family gathering were held at Edna's folk's church and home. It was quite a gathering.

The bar/pool/billiard area was completed by Thanksgiving. A huge neon sign overhung the entrance:

JIM'S PLACE

POOL-BILLIARDS-BEER-DRINKS-FOOD

The thirty-foot hickory bar was the prominent fixture. The bar stools were heavy oak. The beer glasses were large, fourteen-ounce capacity. Twenty-ounce mugs were also available. A refrigeration system in the bar included space for beverages as well as the makings for cold sandwiches. Three tap beers were available, the barrels being located in the basement. Every punchboard on the market was displayed in the bar. A Wurlitzer Nickelodeon, lights blinking and whirling, sat in one corner, ready to be played. A small raised stage sat against the front wall, an upright piano at its one end. Jim had entertainment planned for opening day and night the Saturday after Thanksgiving and every Saturday night thereafter, to draw the crowds. The grand opening was a blast, one free beer per person, a buffet of snacks, free access to the pool and billiard tables. Three different small bands provided the entertainment, all swing combos, one over the noon hour, one over the supper hour, one till closing. IT WAS A BLAST!!!!!!!!! Edna hired a babysitter for the day, sneaking back to the apartment to nurse Frank, on schedule. Four people were hired for all day. The snack buffet was never out of food. The taps never went dry. Every drink in "OLD MR.BOSTON"S *Deluxe Official Bartenders Guide* was available on request. Jim did not run out of a single bar item. It was a warm day for late November. The windows and doors were all open to let out the body heat. The music could be heard up and down Main Street. People danced on the sidewalk. Obviously, Fessenden needed a little fun, and Jim and Edna were going to give it to them. The dry cleaning shop took several more months to get started. Jim had a special sign made for the dry cleaners entrance. His plan was to pick up dry cleaning at numerous spots throughout the county. That was going to be Jim's morning job. He contracted with a small grocery store in all of the towns in the county, Chasley, Bowden, Heaton, Sykeston, Cathay, Emrick, Manfred, Heimdal, Wellsburg, Hamberg and Breman. He skipped Harvey. They already had two dry cleaning firms of their own. But Jim was determined to get some of their business away from them. They did not have pick-up routes until Jim started his. Jim's window signs at the grocery stores out did his competitors. Jim picked up from his spots in the southern part of the county on Mondays and Thursdays, from the northern part on Tuesdays and Fridays, leaving Wednesdays to catch up at his Fesseden shop. He would leave Fesseden at 7:00AM, and be back at the shop at 9:00 to 9:30. He would spend the rest of the morning, at times in the afternoon, cleaning and pressing garments. Edna would open up the bar at 11:00AM with Frank in a basket beside her, staying on duty till Jim finished an early afternoon nap. He would stay in the bar until closing time, 1:00AM. It was a crowded life. Sundays were for cleaning home and shop. Edna kept her faith, attending church every Sunday passively.

CHAPTER TWENTY ONE

Jim shut down the dry cleaning shop for a week in January, hired an old man in town to run the bar and pool hall and took off to Canada with his fishing buddies to do some spearing. After several days to learn the tricks and skills of the sport they ended up hauling some monster northern pike out of the lake. The largest was 24 pounds. Jim hired the same man to help him out in February when Edna took off a week to visit her family. The winter was cold, windy, the thermometer dipping to minus 30 degrees twice and the wind reaching 40 miles and hour several times. The fall had been dry. The strong winds put heavy amounts of dirt into the air. Jim never made his routes those days and few customers made it to the bar, only the thirstiest. Spring brought rains. Prairie flowers colored the roadsides. The North Dakota State flower, the wild rose, was particularly prevalent in its sublime way, persistent beyond the ravages of man and his agricultural abuses of the prairie. Jim noticed nature as he drove his routes. He noticed the migratory waterfowl appear on the potholes, the males of all species displaying their colorfully gaudy mating plumage. The drake pintail was his favorite, brown head, glossed iridescently with purplish pink and green, sharply cut white vestment covering his breast and a long neck front, his back covered with gray and black feathers vermiculated in white. His shoulder feathers were draped like epaulets, black tail coming to a pinpoint, thereof his name. The wing speculum was distinct to his species, colored violet, bronze and green, bordered behind with black then white bars and in front by cinnamon buff bars. His appearance qualified him to attend the most regal of ceremonies, while nearby would be swimming his drab, tan colored mate. These drives to pick up and deliver dry cleaning were never a bore to Jim. These were happy jaunts. Jim drove the Phaeton with the front curtains off, spring air blowing through his hair. He waved to farmers in the fields, most of them known to his business. Some farm ladies would be standing by their mailboxes, knowing the time he would drive by, to hale him down with dirty clothes they needed to have cleaned and back in two days. He would always accommodate them. Jim spread good cheer at his stops in the grocery stores and the proprietors appreciated the little extra income from their commission on the dry cleaning.

Jim had been somewhat aloof to Frank James. His reasoning, it was a mother's realm to attend to and bond with a newborn baby. But as the baby grew and started smiling to attention, developing a personality, then Jim did more than just lean over the basket and mimic Frank James. Jim would pick him up, hoist him above his head and pretend he was going to drop him and thereby arouse him to giggle. Edna had a large rocking chair in the apartment. Jim would end playtime by rocking Frank James to sleep. He would often stay there while Jim took his own afternoon nap. After naptime, Frank James would be Edna's while Jim took over the bar and pool/billiard shift until closing.

CHAPTER TWENTY TWO

The fishing trip to Big Quill Lake in Canada materialized again the summer of 1935. It was another fisherman's success, but tragedy struck the camp the last day Jim and his buddies were on the lake. Jim's group had two round bottom cedar strip wooden boats. Only one boat had an outboard motor, on open fly wheeled Evinrude, 5-horse power. The motored boat towed the other boat. That was the conventional system at the fishing camp on Big Quill Lake for parties of four men. Jim and his buddies were at the far end of the lake mid-afternoon, with more fish in their ice boxes than they needed, in fact had been talking about calling it quits for the day and getting back to the camp. Suddenly a huge five-mile high summer thunderhead had developed in the west. Jim was in the boat with the motor. He pulled over to the other boat, called their attention to the darkening sky in the west and said, "Let's head for camp." He threw the other boat the towrope and headed down the lake. They had hardly gone a mile when the edge of the rapidly moving storm hit them. Waves of severe height developed quickly. Jim could see they were in jeopardy from the waves washing over the transom, more so for the boat they were towing. There were no life preservers in the boats. None of the four were great swimmers. Rain proceeded to fall, in sheets, quickly deepening the water in the boats, further lowering the level of the gunwales to the waves. Earlier in the afternoon it had been noticed that one other four-man group, from the same camp that Jim and his friends were out of, had been fishing further up the lake. Jim's group now saw them also heading down the lake a short distance behind, then the heavy rainfall obscured them from Jim and his buddies. Ahead of Jim a short distance lay an island, dead center in the lake. Jim figured to try and pull in on the leeward side would be his best bet. Jim worried about the boat in tow whipping in the wind as they came around the corner of the island. He had his partner shorten the towrope to bring the towed boat up close. Jim cut the corner short, quickly bringing both boats into the lee of the island. In two minutes the two boats were beached and the four fishermen were on land. What a relief. They scouted the water off the island for the other two boats behind them, but never sighted them. The storm subsided within an hour; they bailed out their boats and headed back to camp, arriving about 5:00PM, well in time for a few drinks before dinner. The proprietor of the camp asked Jim about his group and if they had seen anything of another group who were not back in camp yet. Jim said, "Yes, they had sighted them coming down the lake behind, just when the heavy rain hit, but had not seen them after that". Everyone was fearful of what may have happened to the other group. The proprietor went out on the lake to look for them but darkness ended his search. Jim and his group were scheduled to leave early in the morning, but stayed to join searchers, all hoping the missing group was stranded on shore somewhere without motor power or oars to return to camp. Mid-morning both boats were found, capsized, blown up on shore at the far lower end of the lake. Jim and his group left that noon. They later found the bodies of the four men one week later, when they surfaced from bloating. All four were married men, from Williston, North Dakota, with small children. What a tragedy. It got Jim thinking about the dangers of being on water, not better equipped.

CHAPTER TWENTY THREE

That fall, Frank James started pulling himself up alongside chairs to a standing position. I wasn't long before he was taking a few steps by himself, as a beginner, falling many times, but not discouraged to keep trying. By Christmas he was able to walk from the apartment through the dry cleaning section and into the bar. If Jim heard the patter of Frank James little feet as he approached the bar room door, Jim would hide behind the door to jump out with a big "Boo!" when Frank James came through the door, responding with a jubilant laugh. Jim would then hoist Frank James up on the bar for all the patrons to admire. If Edna did not come to the bar soon to retrieve Frank James, Jim would return him to the apartment. This became a ritual, loved by both Jim and Frank James. The child's vocabulary had enlarged beyond "Mama and Dada". One of his early words was "Beer". Another early one was "Pool". "Dry cleaning" could not be mastered early on, too many syllables. His first recognizable pronunciation was "Rykeening." Jim and Frank James became closer and closer, the little boy a shadow and mimic of his father. That next summer, at age two, he rode with his father on the four a week morning, dry cleaning pickups. Jim had bought a small folding chair to place on the front passenger seat, giving Frank James a view of the countryside. Frank James' vocabulary further expanded, "Cow, horse, barn, wheat, flax, grain shock (gwain sock). He learned the names of all the grocery store employees along the route, greeting them each happily as he walked in the store with Jim.

That fall Jim did some pheasant hunting around Fessenden, but no duck hunting. He spent what little spare time he had on improving the garage for his and Edna's cars, tearing down the old shack they had been using and building a new structure, large enough for both cars and some storage space in front of the cars, as well as on top of the rafters. He hired a carpenter to help him. They made the floor of poured concrete. They insulated the walls and roof so it was warm enough for the cars to start on cold winter mornings. All parts of the business were doing well. Jim hired a lady to help in the dry cleaning shop, serving walk-in customers and doing the pressing. Edna still helped some, but Frank James was requiring more and more of her attention. Jim, Edna and Frank James spent the holidays with Jim's family or Edna's family, as well as some Sundays, which would be about the only Sundays that Edna would miss Sunday church service. Jim and Frank James had Sunday mornings to themselves. Frank James relished Jim reading the Sunday comics to him. Jim added many details to the stories. *THE KATZENJAMMER KIDS* was Frank James favorite. Jim's glorified reading of *TOONERVILLE TROLLEY* was equally exciting.

CHAPTER TWENTY FOUR

Christmas, 1934, was a three-day visit to the Doyers. Jim had his helper take over the place at noon Christmas Eve Day so the Jim Doyer family arrived at the farm mid afternoon. Everyone was in a festive spirit. Liquor, wine and beer were set out for each to make their own choice late afternoon. Christmas Eve dinner was the traditional lutefisk and lefse with meatballs and gravy for the less devoted. Presents under the tree were opened after dinner. Jim was less generous than in the past, now that he had his own family. But he did not hold back for Edna, she receiving a twenty-inch natural pearl necklace. Christmas Day saw a huge roasted turkey set at Lee's end of the table. He carved it like a surgeon. Other traditional dishes included, mashed potatoes, squash baked in butter and brown sugar, pecan dressing, cranberry sauce, fresh rolls and minced pie alamode. The men quickly fell asleep in their chairs while the women washed the dishes.

Frank James was supposed to be taking a nap when he wandered out of the bedroom, whimpering and tugging at his right ear. He felt warm to touch. There was not a thermometer in the house. He had always been so healthy, but the last two days he had the sniffles. Edna was concerned, saying "We are going to Fessenden right away. I am going to see if I can get Doc Hersonford to look at Frank James yet tonight. Frank James complained of pain, "It hurts" all the way back. Edna called the Doc. He came to the house about 7:00PM. He examined the ear with his head mirror, and unshaded table lamp and an ear speculum. His comment was, "Frank James sure has a hot ear. The eardrum is red and bulging. Edna, do you have sweet oil and a hot water bottle? "Yes I do", said Edna. Doc ordered Edna to warm the oil, testing it on the back of her hand to assure its not being too hot, put two drops in Frank James ear every

171

two hours, all night long with the hot water bottle on his ear constantly, that also not too hot, covered with a towel. He also said that a little aspirin would be ok. His final remark when he left the house was, "Bring him into my office tomorrow morning at 9:00. If the ear is not better, I may have to lance the eardrum." During the night the pain in Frank James ear relented. He slept soundly. However, Edna noticed in the morning that there was a spot of bloody stain on Frank James pillow. She took him to Doc's office, telling Doc of the bloody spot. He looked at Frank James ear saying, "The eardrum is ruptured. Pus is running out. I wish we had that new medicine discovered in Germany, sulfanilamide. They say it works wonders. Stop your sweet oil, Edna. Has he vomited? Edna answered, "No" Doc said, "Make him take lots of fluids. Do not plug up the ear with cotton. Let it run. Call me if there is any trouble." Edna said "Thanks a million, Doc."

Frank James was quite good that day. Jim came back from the bar often to try and jolly his little boy. Frank James ate some food and drank a gallon of fresh squeezed orange juice. His temperature stayed down. The ear drained profusely, thick yellow pus. He slept well that night. Next morning his appetite was not good. Edna took his temperature. It was 103 degrees. He vomited three times, some of it food from supper the night before. He said, "My head hurts! I want to lay down." He was still sleeping at noon. Edna tried to awaken him. She could barely arouse him. She called Doc Hersonford immediately. He came to the apartment at noon. He listened to Frank James chest. He said, "His lungs are clear. He does not have pneumonia." Next he placed his one hand under Frank James head and lifted him up. Frank James neck was stiff as a board. He turned to Edna, "Frank James has spinal meningitis. This is bad." Edna had heard of a child in the country near Fessenden die from spinal meningitis the week before. She said, "O My God!" The lady helping in the dry cleaning shop was standing nearby. Edna told her to go get Jim from the bar. He came quickly, leaving the lady helper to tend the customers. Doc said, "Jim your boy is very, very sick." Jim said, "Is there anything you can do? Should he be in the hospital?" Doc said, "There is no more to do in the hospital then here. I will call nurse Luella Kvaley to come over right away. She will stay till midnight. I will find another special nurse to take over at midnight. Miss Kvaley is very excellent, very experienced." The word was out around town immediately about Jim and Edna's little boy having meningitis. The County Health Officer tacked a quarantine sign on Doyer's house that afternoon. The minister from Edna's church stopped mid-afternoon. Jim went back to the bar room only briefly, telephoning his dependable helper to come over and take over. Edna telephoned her folks. Jim telephoned his. They were advised to not visit because of the quarantine.

Frank James was in a deep coma by midnight, no longer taking even sips of water. The nurse called the doctor. He came right away. At 2:00AM Frank James breathing became very shallow. He died in the dark of night at 2:15AM. Jim and Edna both fell to their knees by Frank James bed, putting their heads down on his little, motionless body, still warm, but with no life. They both sobbed deeply. The minister had been called. When he arrived he asked Jim and Edna to fold their hands. They prayed the Lord's Prayer together, then the minister prayed to the Lord to take Frank James to Heaven and for the Lord to comfort Jim and Edna in their deep sorrow and to give them strength to rise above their grief and to carry on the work assigned to them in life and to derive strength from their love for each other. The undertaker came shortly after, wrapping Frank James in his blankets and carrying him out the door to his car. Because of the quarantine, certain cautions were required in regards to the burial being no longer than one day after death and the casket not being open for viewing.

Jim and Edna and their families were able to view Frank James at the funeral home the next day. He looked so sweet, not the expression of death, but rather as though he was sleeping. Jim was tempted to pick him up and toss him in the air as he had done many times to make Frank James giggle. Instead Jim stood with his arm around Edna while the two sobbed together. Everybody was wiping tears from their eyes. JIM"S PLACE was closed the next day for the funeral. People not even knowing the Doyers attended it. A fire had been prepared the afternoon on top of the gravesite. Two gravediggers had taken turns keeping the fire hot all night to soften the frozen ground so they could dig the grave the next morning. The saddest part of the day was the graveside ceremony. It was a bright day, the low sun glistening off the snow covered landscape and no wind to muffle the words of the pastor. "Ashes to Ashes, Dust to Dust" as he sprinkled a small vial of earth on the little casket, which was immediately lowered into the grave. Jim and Edna didn't want to leave the gravesite. They were having a terrible time accepting that Frank James was no longer with them in body, just in spirit. The reception at the church, to include a small lunch of cake, cookies and coffee, was equally difficult. Jim and Edna found it nearly impossible to talk to people about the loss of their Frank James. What reason was there for such a loss? Jim wondered if it was a form of punishment placed upon him, certainly not on Frank James, so little and innocent. Jim begged the Lord for forgiveness for all his wrongdoings, somehow thinking that would bring Frank James back.

CHAPTER TWENTY FIVE

Jim and Edna both had trouble sleeping. Jim took to drinking whiskey at night, knocking himself out so he would sleep. He even took several shots in the afternoon to take his mind off Frank James. Edna did not approve of this much drinking. She was not a heavy drinker herself. After several months, Jim quit all together. He became sullen, talking very little to Edna, his help or his customers or his and Edna's families. He was down in the dumps. Edna was fearful of his developing mental illness. He remained morose through the next summer. Edna was so hoping Jim would go fishing with his buddies. They asked him, begged him. He would not go. He did not go hunting that fall. It was difficult to get him to smile. He lost weight. He just lay around on Sundays. Edna was fearful for his health. When he went to bed at night, he would quietly lay on his side, purposely not touching Edna. She would try and snuggle up to him. He offered no response, totally withdrawn. This behavior persisted month after month, through the winter. He started to come to life in the late spring. By summer he was nearly himself again. That was a long period of mourning. He went fishing with his gang that summer, 1937.

CHAPTER TWENTY SIX

Edna became pregnant that fall. It was a joy to both Jim and Edna. As the months went by they looked forward to her date of confinement, which was expected to be in mid July, near Frank James birthday. Edna entered the hospital at 2:00AM on July 15th and delivered a boy two hours later. He was immediately named John David. John was Lee's second name. David was Edna's father's second name. The baptism three weeks later was a joyous affair. Jim was very happy about his newborn son but in a different way than he had been with Frank James. He did not establish a strong bond. There was a reluctance to become too emotionally attached. He tended to allow Edna to keep that role to herself. Jim never tried to break the mother/son attachment. Jim kept involved nearly 100% in his business. He did start to drink again but sporadically, not every night. Probably no more often than once every month he would start drinking on Saturday night, then continue on Sunday till he was stone drunk, then crawl to bed and sleep it off by Monday morning. This developed into a pattern that Edna could predict. She expressed her concerns to Jim about these bouts and he shrugged it off. There never was any meanness on Jim's part and certainly never any physical or verbal abuse. Jim loved Edna too much for that and her love for Jim continued strong. Jim's lack of attachment to John David was not aggressively intentional. It was part of his inner response to the loss of his little buddy Frank James.

CHAPTER TWENTY SEVEN

Life went forward in Fessenden, North Dakota. Both the bar and pool hall and the dry cleaning businesses continued to grow. Jim kept the place attractive, updated the amenities regularly, made sure he had popular entertainment on Saturday nights and ran a respectable place of business. Anyone getting out of line with their drinking or their behavior got the boot and were told not to try and return. He formed several Billiard/Pool Leagues offering prizes of value. The idea of happy hour may have had its beginning in Fessenden, North Dakota. Drinks and beer one half price from 5:00 to 7:00 on Monday, Tuesday and Wednesday evenings. Supposedly the slowest nights of the week turned into the busiest. Jim's interest in hunting and fishing fell off. He kept his nose to the grindstone.

Edna's parents met a tragic death in January 1939. They were heading from their farm to Williston for a day of shopping and to take in an afternoon show at the Hollywood Movie Theater. Edna's folks were heading west, about half way to Williston, when a truck heading east suddenly went out of control on the ice, swerving into the couples lane. It was an explosive head on collision. A driver in a car some distance behind witnessed the accident. The truck driver and Edna's parents were killed instantly. Both of Edna's parents were young, in there fifties. Edna faced the tragedy well. Jim handled it poorly. An older brother of Edna's had been farming with his dad. He was able to take over the farm operation.

The late thirties and early Forties saw prosperity return to the United States. The prices of farmland and commodity prices did benefit. The land Jim bought in Wisconsin, still in Priscella's name, became worth something. Priscella wanted to sign it over to Jim. He refused, insisting it was hers. She sold it for a good price, giving a good share of the returns to the Fessenden Community Library for construction of a new wing, known as the Frank James Doyer Memorial Wing. Jim did not attend the commemoration ceremony. He knew he would break down and cause a scene. The rest of both Jim and Edna's families were all there. Coffee and cookies were served after the ceremony. Jim cried when Edna told him about it later.

December 7th, 1941 changed life in the US. It was Sunday, JIM"S PLACE closed. Edna was ready to go to MERT'S CAFÉ, a block away, for the well-known Sunday Brunch Spread. Edna cooked at home very little. She had been working more and more in the business and did not need the burden of fixing meals. She had been trying to talk Jim into going with her, saying "Getting out will be good for you, better than what's in that bottle of Jim Crow." When Jim had heard the news of the bombing he had started to weep. When Edna saw that she insisted that Jim go with her and John David. She wasn't going to leave him home to cry in his booze. The café was abuzz with the news of the Jap's dastardly act. If there had been a recruiting officer in the place he could have signed up an entire company of infantry. It was good Edna had taken Jim with her. It perked him up. Jim did not drink anymore that day when they returned to the apartment. He kept his ear glued to the radio. Next day Jim bought a new radio for the bar, a big floor model with three speakers in it. Nobody wanted to miss the news, particularly President Roosevelt's address to the nation and Congress's declaration of war the next day, Monday December 8th, 1941. JIM'S PLACE was full that day, beer drinkers shouting epithets against the Jap's, cheering Roosevelt and Congress. Many young men drove to Minot that week to sign up for the Marines, bypassing the draft. It was a new path of life in the United States. Over the next few months, many middle-aged families migrated to California where high paying defense work was available. North Dakota towns without industry were left out. There seemed to be little glory in raising wheat and fattening cattle, the plainsman's role of filling the bread basket of the world, but many of them stuck to their meager role and were proud of their accomplishments. If the US Army declared them 4F, unfit medically for military service, they could still farm.

CHAPTER TWENTY EIGHT

John David started playing pool before he started school. He had the dexterity required to be a good player. He would take on adults of long experience and beat them easily. He used an empty beer bottle case to stand on. Such adult like behavior by a small child was entertaining. People came from long distances to play him and feel privileged to be beaten. He was a bright child but not stuck on himself nor did he have any high opinion of himself. He was just a sweet, outgoing kid. John David's mother, being an ex teacher recognized his braininess and made efforts to cultivate it, having him read books in advance of his age, do mathematic problems, make change for customers and write letters to his kin. John was more than ready for kindergarten the fall after his fifth birthday. He was physically large for his age but never used his advantage to bully the other children. He was helpful rather than overbearing. School achievement came easy for John. He was at the top of his class.

Jim had not taken John with him on his dry cleaning route. Being with Edna was better for him. As John became older he went fishing with his father and mother occasionally. They were Sunday trips to nearby lakes or stock ponds. They were thrilling excursions to John. Catches would be limited to pan fish. No matter how small the fish were, they tasted delicious. Picnic lunch at a weathered old picnic table in the shade of a cottonwood tree was the ultimate. John continued to achieve academically in grade school and high school. He was a good athlete, playing on the major sports teams. His fame as a pool player was locally renown. Very rarely would anyone beat him. Even as John matured to adulthood, misuse of liquor was no temptation to him. He saw enough of that in his father's weekly debauches. John had widespread freedom with his social life, no interference from father and total trust on the part of mother. He was a handsome young man, popular with the girls and admired by his male contemporaries. As soon as he obtained his drivers license, at age fifteen, he had privileges to use one of the two family cars, usually Edna's. Of course, this increased his popularity with friends. Edna progressed to never cooking meals at home. Lunch was often at the bar. Dinner was at MERT'S CAFÉ or the local drive-in, BILL'S BURGERS AND MALTS.

Jim's father, Lee, died suddenly in 1955 at the age of seventy-two. He had been failing for several years. Shane moved back home and took over the farm. He and Priscella's husband, Sven, worked cooperatively and enjoyed success. Ann moved to Voltaire into a small house when Lee died, so Shane, his wife and children could take over the home place.

John developed plans to attend college, with no real goal when he matriculated. He chose the University of Iowa. Jim and Edna were supportive, particularly Edna. She had a stronger feeling for higher education than did Jim. John enrolled in the science curriculum. He obtained excellent grades, straight "A's". He pursued his studies seriously. His parent's money was not to be wasted. He did not lazy around during the summers, obtaining jobs of various demands. Before long he established a goal, dentistry. Acceptance into the University of Iowa Dentistry School was no problem. He met a charming young U of Iowa co-ed with whom he fell in love. They were married while John was still in school. Their first child was a daughter.

Jim became very ill during John's final year in Dental School. He developed irreversible congestive heart failure, at least in part related to his alcohol consumption. He died suddenly a few months later at the age of fifty-five years. He did not live to realize the pride of seeing his son, John, receive his Doctorate of Dental Surgery Degree. Though not overtly expressive of his pride, Jim had admired John's

181

academic accomplishment. John David always felt this to have been a vacant moment in his life, his father being absent at the commencement exercise at the University of Iowa that spring. It did not, however, mar his life.

CHAPTER TEWNTY-NINE

John had looked at several locations to practice dentistry prior to his graduation. He was most attracted to a city in southern Nebraska, population 4000, strongly Norwegian in heritage. The city had several dentists, one wanting to fully retire. John took over his practice. John and his wife immediately became engaged in community activities. John was popular as a skilled dentist. John's wife bore him two sons within a few years. As the sons grew, John supported their interest in sports, Boy scouts and other pastimes of youth. John was very active in the Chamber of Commerce activities and a leader in the local Kiwanis Club. He loved to fish the cold waters of Canada, including his family on his trips, mainly his sons and subsequently his son-in-law. He become the leader of a group of men who traveled far north into Canada every summer on a grand fishing trip to lure numerous, monstrous northern pike and walleyed pike to their boats. John was a very proud grandfather when his daughter brought her first daughter into the world. Family was important to John David. John always had a smile on his face, ever exuding happiness. He transferred this to those around him. No one avoided his company. He was a pleasure to be with. Everyone liked John Doyer.

Edna ran JIM"S PLACE by herself after Jim died, hiring more help. She took a second husband, a retired telephone lineman. They subsequently sold the business, bought a motor home, traveled and enjoyed other leisurely pursuits till that became a burden. They then gave John the motor home. Edna died suddenly after a few years. Her second husband lives on. John's father-in-law died quite young and his children never knew either of their grandfathers.

EPILOGUE

Life for Jim (Clutch) Doyer's descendants proved to be much different than for himself, more organized and conventional, certainly less threatening, maybe less exciting. To say whose lives were more or less productive could be argued. To say Jim's life was less acceptable socially would depend on how it was equated to the time of his life, the years in the twentieth century in which he lived. There is no question, those years of the 1920's and 1930's were driven by much different forces and mores than the years of the second half of the twentieth century. Some people may yearn for the old days; some may celebrate their passage. Regardless, they are gone, Jim and his counterparts gone also, remembered in the tales of this story. It was a delight to join them in their golden days, sad to share their sorrows, to be aghast when they took revenge, to feel them breathe, slowly bring them into vision, to hear their voices drift by, to be near them.